Mute

of

Pendywick Place

And the Torn Page

A

Victorian

Mystery Series

by

Alydia Rackham

ALYDIA RACKHAM

ISBN: 1535294019
ISBN-13: 978-1535294010

For my faithful Patreon readers,

My family, and Jaicee.

"The biggest problem in communication
is the illusion that it has taken place."

-George Bernard Shaw

Chapter One

London

November 3rd

1881

Fog.

Lurking in low, thick clouds around the faces of the buildings that lined Brompton Road. Loitering in doorways, veiling windows. Chilling the feet of the men who walked the paving with crisp steps and bowed heads. Swirling around the black skirts of the ladies who reluctantly shut ringing shop doors behind them as they ventured out into the gloom. Parting like a ghostly river before the clatter of the hansom horse; hanging in a wake behind the driver's battered top hat and cloaked shoulders. Stifling the throbbing orange street lamps beneath shrouds of cobweb.

She perched on the curb of the walkway, glancing up and down the broad street. As she paused, a disembodied bell in some nearby tower voiced five haunting, identical notes. She drew herself up, gripped her small, light bag tighter in her gloved hand. She held her breath, waiting for any clamor of a cab heading toward her through the wall of mist.

Nothing but a distant trundle of an omnibus. So she braced herself again, stepped off the curb, and onto the cobbles.

Her shoes clapped against the damp, slick stones as she lifted her skirt and picked up her pace. She fixed her gaze on the place where the far walkway should be, listening intently...

She hopped up onto the opposing curb, spun and faced the street.

She could not see the spot from whence she had just come. Biting the inside of her cheek, she turned to the left, and headed up the walk.

Each time she crossed a narrow street that turned left to abandon the main road, she counted it. She did not meet the eyes of any of the finely-dressed ladies or bowler-hatted gentlemen she passed, but set her mouth and walked quicker. Her skirts rustled with her swift movement, and she ignored the cold in her feet as she splashed through puddles.

Finally, She trotted out into the center of a little lane that wove off into the forest of buildings. She stared down the narrow passage, reflexively searched for a street sign...

Stopped herself, and attended to the lane again.

Darkness was falling, and shadows thickening. Ahead of her, a few street lamps burned like candles in a cavern, dripping measly pools of light down around their bases.

She started forward. Her footsteps rang louder here. She cast up and around her at what she could see of the clean facades of the houses—the neatly-painted doors, the trimmed windows...

Again, She counted. Knockers, this time. Squeezing the handle of her luggage.

...seven, eight, nine, ten...

Lamps glowed in several of the windows, like smudges against the frosty glass. Far ahead, she glimpsed a few other murky pedestrians, but none ventured down this way.

...twenty, twenty-one, twenty-two, twenty-three...

Her chest tensed, her pulse picking up as she quickened her pace...

She slowed, and stopped, letting out her tight breath in a cloud.

The twenty-sixth house, on her left.

The bricks distinguished it right away—deep red, almost brown—in sharp contrast to the pale houses on either side. This darker house seemed to resent even having to touch shoulders with the others—it was so severely narrow, and stretched up a full story taller than its neighbors. Ivy masked half its face. The fog prowled around the front steps of this house like an old, protective dog.

aside and stepped up next to Mr. Cutworth. She had a stern mouth and flushed face, but bright brown eyes that captured Hers straightaway. Mrs. Butterfield gave Her a quick glance up and down—one that felt entirely different from Mr. Cutworth's—and pulled the door open to its entirety.

"She is clearly not a button seller, Mr. Cutworth," Mrs. Butterfield admonished sharply. "Has she told you her name?"

"Not a word," Mr. Cutworth replied. "She seems entirely befuddled—must be a vagabond."

"Has it occurred to you that she might have some defect, some impediment that prevents her from answering you?" Mrs. Butterfield inquired, putting a fist on her hip. "Perhaps she is deaf! Or perhaps she does not even speak English!"

Mr. Cutworth's face colored.

"We have all manner and sort stopping by this door, Mr. Cutworth," Mrs. Butterfield continued. "But in all my years, I have never happened upon a deaf, vagabond button-seller."

The whole of Mr. Cutworth's face turned completely red now. He straightened his waistcoat, and turned from the door.

"I will leave her in your capable hands, then," he decided, and swiftly departed into the house. Mrs. Butterfield heaved a sigh, and turned back to Her.

"You'll have to forgive us, Miss. We've newly hired a

butler, and he isn't accustomed to the sort of folk that usually arrive uninvited to Pendywick Place."

In answer, She nodded quickly.

"Ah, so you *can* understand English!" Mrs. Butterfield smiled. "But you *do* have business with Mr. Collingwood, then?"

Again, She nodded quickly—even harder.

"Then come in, come in, before you catch your death." Mrs. Butterfield stepped aside and beckoned to her. Quickly, She stepped across the threshold, and into the entryway. Mrs. Butterfield closed the door behind her with a resounding clap, then bustled past Her.

"Please wait right here while I announce you."

She watched Mrs. Butterfield trundle across the pale beaten rug toward the other door at the far end. The housekeeper opened it, hurried through and shut it—

But it did not latch.

Biting her lip, She moved her bag to grasp it in both hands, and glanced around at the dark-wood entryway, lit by a single lamp to her left. On the right hand wall hung several long coats, three hats; and her attention caught on two very unusual walking sticks that waited next to the umbrella in the stand in the corner. They seemed to be made of rough-hewn blackthorn wood, polished till they shone.

Voices. Low, furtive.

Mrs. Butterfield's first.

Then...

Another.

Holding her breath, She crept forward, hoping she would not make the floor creak beneath her shoes. She paused just a few feet from the door, leaning forward and listening...

"A woman? What kind of woman?"

A man's voice. Like a rumble of thunder—yet precise as a scalpel.

"A *young* woman, sir," came Mrs. Butterfield's hushed answer. "I should say perhaps twenty-three."

"Who is she?" that deep, penetrating voice again. A winter wind of a voice.

"She didn't say, sir."

"Didn't or couldn't?" he demanded.

"I don't know, sir."

"Well, what does she look like?" he pressed.

"Medium height; she's wearing a red dress that's in rather poor condition, a long black coat that was probably her mother's, and a blue straw hat," Mrs. Butterfield told him. "She's got a pretty face, black eyes. Although I must say she looks a deal too pale, and a bit on the thin side. Very black hair, too. Only one piece of small luggage."

"You don't know her?"

"Never seen her before in my life, sir," she said.

The man let out a labored sigh.

"Very well, then, show her in. I've had about enough of Milton for this half of my lifetime, anyhow."

The door suddenly swung open. She jumped back as

Mrs. Butterfield stuck her head around and smiled at her.

"Do come in."

She nodded, trying not to shiver, and stepped past Mrs. Butterfield.

"May I present Mr. Basil Collingwood," Mrs. Butterfield announced. Then, the housekeeper curtsied, and bustled off through a doorway to the left, leaving Her alone.

The dusty scent of books filled Her nose and throat. Frowning, she cast a glance through the well-lit, backward-L-shaped room. Off to her far right and nearly behind her, three armchairs crowded with pillows cornered a low, knick-knack-laden fireplace and mantel, forming a small, cluttered parlor; ahead of her and to the right stood a chestnut-colored piano buried beneath stacks of books and papers. Beyond that waited a desk laden with a shiny typewriter, glowing lamp, more books, several pens, a few portraits, and a pile of blank paper. All the walls round about were composed of shelves, crammed floor to ceiling with all sizes of books. Everything was lit by a chandelier that hung over the desk, as well as lamps on iron sconces that clung to the corners of the bookshelves.

Directly in front of her, a red-carpeted staircase marched straight up and away, then abruptly turned to the right and vanished into the next story. The wall this created before her also cradled a wide, thick bookshelf...

Her fingers slackened on her baggage, and she stared.

A young man sat on top of this bookshelf.

He leaned back against a thick pillar, and stretched his

long legs out across the top of the shelf. He wore only coal-colored trousers, stockings, a shirt and grey waistcoat—no coat or shoes or tie. He held a cumbersome old book up in front of him, a set of brass, round-rimmed reading glasses resting on the end of his nose. Right beside his left shoulder, a lamp protruded from the pillar, illuminating the pages, as well as his angular, white, striking face, and short, curly dark hair. He turned his head. Light flashed from his lenses.

He frowned directly down at Her, over the top of his spectacles. A terrible, dark, stormy brow—eyes grey as frost caught in the morning sun.

"So you won't tell Mrs. Butterfield your name," he stated—his bass tones vibrated through Her marrow. "But you understand English and you're not deaf."

She nodded, clenching her jaw, feeling all her muscles go cold.

"Is your identity some sort of secret?" He lifted an eyebrow. "Am I supposed to guess?"

She clutched her bag handle so tightly she feared it might break.

He rolled his eyes, slapped his book shut and swung his legs over the side. He tossed the book down on top of the shelf—it landed with a tremendous *thud*. He pulled off his spectacles and set them on the book, then easily hopped down to the floor. The floorboards squeaked uproariously.

She sucked in her breath, her ribs contracting and her brow twisting as she fought not to turn and run. Even without his shoes, he was a good foot taller than she—lean, yet carelessly graceful. He stuck his hands in his trousers pockets, kicked his head back and strode up to her, eyeing her down his nose.

"So what is it, then?" he asked flatly. "Lisp? Stuttering? Aphemia?"

She frowned up at him, blinking rapidly. He sighed again.

"Come, don't be shy. I've heard every wretched utterance a human mouth can possibly spit out—no mumbling or sputtering that comes from yours has a chance of surprising me."

She stood frozen, fighting to breathe, to keep her head from spinning...

He frowned harder at her, his grey eyes flashing with lightning—cutting down into her heart.

"Are you entirely mute, then?"

She sucked in a sharp breath, her cheeks flushing.

"Ah. All right." He turned crisply, snatched up a piece of paper, a book and a pencil from off the piano, and swooped back toward her.

She flinched back.

"What—What on earth?" he scoffed, instantly stopping and wrinkling his nose at her. "Calm down. I'm not in the habit of attacking people with writing utensils." He arranged the paper on top of the thin book, then held all three things out to her. "Tell me what you want."

She stared at the paper, wide-eyed, her heartbeat accelerating.

Chapter Two

She jerked to a stop.

Sniffed, blinked the water out of her eyes, and quickly glanced around.

Evening had fallen. The fog had thickened so that she could only glimpse the median of the street to her left, but nothing beyond. Ahead of her, a few street lamps throbbed, and the phantoms of coaches, hansoms and horses trundled to and fro.

How far had she come?

She had broken into a run after leaving Pendywick Place, her vision scarlet, and rushed down several alleys and narrow side streets. Now, as she paused on a curb, shocking back to her senses...

She realized she had no idea where she was.

She spun around, searching the shadows behind her.

Nothing looked familiar.

Her breathing picked up, and she tasted the coal dust in the air. She swiped the tears off her face, squeezed her fists...

Gasped. Looked down.

She had left her bag at Pendywick Place.

Panic shot through her chest.

She grabbed her skirts and hurried back the way she had come, heart pounding, fighting to recognize one of the buildings, or a lamp, or a turn...

She kept going, straining against the increasing dark, her shoes slapping on the wet paving...

This way. She had to turn left to head the correct direction—she was certain of it.

She turned a sharp corner and plunged into an alley. Panting, she kept going, aiming for the lamp at the far end...

She kicked a bottle. It thudded against her shoe and skittered off ahead of her across the cobbles, then cracked against a nearby building.

She winced as the racket banged through the slender space, and she slowed down. Her wet skirts swished, her breathing echoed.

"Oi, what 'ave we 'ere?"

She whipped around.

A short figure emerged from a doorway. She could only see his outline—he wore a long coat, far too big for him, and a battered, tilted top-hat. He stuck his hands in his trousers pockets and cocked his head as he sauntered toward her.

"Wut, did you get lost, sweet 'art?" he drawled. "Wut's a lady like you doin' in these parts o' London?"

17

She gritted her teeth, and took two steps back from him. He sounded young, perhaps thirteen. She closed her fists tighter, and kept backing away. And he followed.

"Aow, wut's the 'urry, missus?" he insisted. "Just wanted a friendly chat. Lovely evenin' for it."

She took one more step back, turned to run—

Her shoulder struck something.

The stench of body odor and liquor washed over her. She leaped back.

A man blocked her path. Stout, broad-shouldered, and thick—he wore a crooked hat, too. She couldn't see any more of his features—he loomed a black shadow over her.

A savage snarl sounded from around his knees. Her gaze darted down to find a small, muscular white dog baring its fangs at her.

"Easy, Bullseye," the man soothed, his voice coarse and deep. He turned and looked at Her, and she could feel his gaze burning through her.

"We don't want no trouble, Missus," the man purred. "Just so long as you 'and over yer valuables."

She shook her head.

He lunged at her. Grabbed her by both wrists and jerked her toward him—clamped down so hard she felt her bones come together.

She bared her teeth, but made no sound.

"Ah, yer a good girl for not screamin'," he breathed his rancid breath in her face.

The next moment, she felt a second set of quick hands

feel her all over, and dip into her coat pockets.

"She ain't got nothin' we want, Mr. Sikes," the boy declared.

She felt Sikes grin.

"Oh, yes she do." And he slammed her back against the wall.

Her breath slapped out of her lungs. Her vision went black. With one hand, Mr. Sikes covered her mouth, and with the other he shoved in past her coat and wrapped his arm around her waist.

CRACK.

A sound like splitting sapling.

Sikes staggered, his head dipping. He released Her— her feet hit the ground again and she gasped, trying to clear her vision—

Sikes stumbled to the side, turning to face the other end of the alley—

A tall, lean man stood there, in a top-hat. The next second, a stick in his hand flashed like lightning—darted out and slapped Sikes in the side of the head.

Sikes' hand twitched up to grab his own ear—he stared for half a second—then he roared out a long string of curses.

He lunged at the tall man.

The tall man stepped nimbly out of the way, whirled and clouted Sikes in the back of the neck.

Sikes toppled onto his face.

The dog roared and leaped at the tall man.

The tall man crisply clipped it in the nose, sending the

dog howling back. With a sharp, outraged cry, Sikes scrambled up, trying to face the tall man—

The tall man coiled his stick over his shoulder and lashed Sikes in the temple. Sikes crumpled to the street.

Next second, the tall man whipped a revolver from beneath his coat, pivoted and sighted the opposite direction—

Where the boy jerked to a halt, dropped the bottle he held, and lifted both hands in the air.

"Wise decision," the tall man decided. "I would hate to have to shoot you."

She twitched. She knew that voice!

The tall man lifted his chin.

"But, if you come one step closer," he warned, smooth and cold. "That's exactly what I'll do."

"Yes, sir," the boy stammered.

"Off you go," the tall man said. The boy dropped his arms, turned and ran.

The tall man tucked his gun back in his coat, took his stick in his left hand, and stepped up to Her.

"Are you all right?"

Basil. Basil Collingwood.

Her mouth worked, but she made no sound. Finally, she shut her jaw and just nodded, once.

"Come. This is no place for civilized people," Basil muttered, taking her by the arm. He swept her past Sikes, still lying sprawled on the stones, as well as the snarling, whining dog—and out onto the lighted street once more.

He kept hold of her arm as they walked, though he did not grip her, and hustled her down the paving. At last she could see him. He wore a fine, long, fitted black coat, scarf and gloves, and his polished top hat perfectly framed his stormy brow, flashing grey glance and pale, angular profile. She wanted to pull loose of him—but all her muscles still trembled too badly. She could hear other people traipsing back and forth on the other side of the street, but still could not make out their shapes. She battled to gather her wits, calm her raging heartbeat—

Movement up ahead.

A medium-sized dog darted out of an alley, stopped, saw them and pricked up its ears. It had an intelligent, foxlike face, a curled tail, slender body and limbs—and it was the most unusual blond color. It had bright gold eyes with black around them, almost like Egyptian kohl.

It wagged its tail, and trotted toward them.

"Hullo, Jack," Basil greeted the dog, slowing their pace to a stop. Jack quickly sniffed Her skirts, glancing sideways up at her as he did.

"I would introduce you, but the lady seems disinclined to share her information with me," Basil remarked flatly.

21

She watched the dog carefully, daring to put her hand down to touch his head...

He let her, continuing his inspection.

"Jack assisted me in finding you," Basil explained offhand, taking up his stick, letting go of her and starting forward again. "But I wouldn't let him follow me entirely because I knew there was a bulldog in that alley. Jack would fight, of course, but he isn't remotely equipped to make a contest of it. Rather like yourself."

She ground her teeth and followed after him. Jack hopped out of her way, then pranced easily beside her, catching up to Basil. His claws clicked on the stone in rhythm to Basil's walking stick.

"I'd like to know exactly what you were thinking of, taking off by yourself in London, all alone, without the slightest idea as to where you were going," Basil said, lengthening his stride so she had to quicken her pace to keep up. "But of course, you're not going to enlighten me, so I ought to have checked my curiosity at the door."

They wound down a few more streets, and She could hear the rising sound of traffic coming from a busy road ahead. Then, he turned down a horseshoe shaped lane...

And before them, just as morose as before, rose Pendywick Place.

"You left your luggage on my floor, along with the mess you made," Basil told her, trotting up his front steps. "And you've made me late to my club." He turned and gave her a sarcastic smile. "You're welcome."

She felt heat rise in her face. He turned back around and pushed through the door. Jack hopped up the steps and darted inside right along with him. She hoisted her skirts and climbed after—and then caught the door as it almost fell shut on her head. She grabbed its edge, her muscles binding up as she wildly considered thrashing it hard back against the inside wall—but she stopped herself.

Instead, she took a deep breath, and trailed after the sound of Basil and Jack clattering through the second door and into the library, where the floorboards screeched under their footsteps.

"Oh, heavens—did you find her?" Mrs. Butterfield cried, hurrying through the door by the staircase. "Gracious, child, I wish you hadn't done that! Gone out into the streets all alone, at this hour!"

She tried to smile at Mrs. Butterfield as she stepped through the second door, but didn't quite manage. Mrs. Butterfield grasped her earnestly by the upper arms and leaned in to look at her.

"Your face is all smeared with soot—and your neck is red! What happened to you?"

"She was accosted by a pair of colorful gentlemen and a dog in a back alley," Basil filled in for her, taking off his hat and smoothing his hair. "So at least we've discovered one thing about her," He gave her a look. "She isn't from Town. Now, Mrs. Butterfield, if you'll get her bag and order a hansom to take her to the train station so she doesn't go wandering off into Shoreditch, I'm sure she'd be much obliged."

Her head came up and She stared at him—but he crisply put his hat back on and turned back toward the door.

"I'm off. I'll need tea at ten o'clock," he barked, and he strode through the second door, leaving Jack behind, his tail wagging faintly as he watched Basil go.

She felt Mrs. Butterfield squeeze her arms, and her head came back around.

"I'll beg pardon from the master later, but I'll do no such thing," she said firmly, her eyes bright. She briskly rubbed her hands up and down Her arms and gave her a smile. "You'll come to the kitchen with me, warm up by the fire, have something to eat, and clean yourself up. Come, Jack," she called, and she urged Her through that side door by the staircase and into a hallway, the dog following behind, perked with interest.

She followed Mrs. Butterfield down the dim corridor, which was lined with portraits, and into a grand dining room, lit by a low chandelier. The table could seat ten people, but it was not set—only a very long, lace tablecloth covered it, and two silver candlesticks with white candles. On the far wall, presiding over the whole room, a tattered, mounted lion's head opened its mouth in a silent roar—though it was missing one top fang.

"That's Leonidas," Mrs. Butterfield commented. "Mr. Collingwood picked him up at an estate sale—said he'd been looking for something to fill that empty space. But I rather think he just felt sorry for the poor thing—he's always been fond of animals of all shapes and sizes."

Mrs. Butterfield kept walking, while She eyed the lion and frowned at the housekeeper's remark.

Ahead of her, Mrs. Butterfield pushed through a swinging door, and so She followed...

Into a charming, well-lit kitchen.

A long table with two chairs sat square in the middle, a ceiling-high cabinet stood in the far corner between two windows, a smaller table with no chairs waited by one range, and copper pots crowded yet another range. The range by the table radiated heat. All the corners and shelves were packed with bowls, pots and pans, jars, bottles and crocks— but everything was clean, tidy and orderly. It smelled like roasted bird, potatoes, and lye soap. Mrs. Butterfield clomped across the wooden floor to the range, waving Her to the table.

"Have a seat, dear, and I'll find what you need."

The dog trotted casually in, following Mrs. Butterfield, watching her every move.

Carefully, She eased down into one of the wooden chairs and watched Mrs. Butterfield open the cabinets and get out the tea things, which clinked as she set them on the counter. She then moved to a large copper tub that hung against the wall, twisted a knob...

And water shot out into her kettle.

Staring, She sat up straight, astonished—and wanted to hurry over and see this phenomenon closer. But no sooner had the kettle filled than Mrs. Butterfield twisted the knob the other way and the water stopped. She then set the kettle on the range with a clank, opened the front of the range and jabbed the fire with a poker.

"Now, I'll get you something to eat whilst you warm up," Mrs. Butterfield sighed, wiping her hands off on her apron. The housekeeper sent Her a smile. "It's nice to have company in the evening time again. We haven't hosted a dinner in this house in an age. I used to have my daughter here, Betsy, but this past summer she got a job at a great house in the country. She's always wanted to see the countryside—poor girl was born in London and always felt stifled by all the coal and the traffic. I'd say she'll be a good sight happier and healthier out there—but that means I hardly ever see her!"

As she talked, Mrs. Butterfield went into the pantry and gathered up a half loaf of bread, a cut of cheddar cheese, some butter and jam, and began preparing them on a plate on the counter. Jack sat down near her, wagged his tail, and licked his lips.

"Mr. Cutworth is a qualified butler to be sure," Mrs. Butterfield went on. "But he keeps to himself in his off hours, reading in his room and taking his meals there too, and isn't talkative during the day. And Mr. Collingwood, well—you have seen how he is." The kettle whistled. She snatched it off the range and poured the steaming water into the teapot. "He's popular enough with his friends and professors from Oxford, and men who share the same profession—he's highly respected for his research. And he's brilliant, of course. Written eleven books, and he isn't yet thirty years old! And several articles and papers for respected journals, besides. And he has many patients who come to him for help with their speech impediments, that haven't had any luck anywhere else." Mrs. Butterfield turned and handed a small piece of cheese down to Jack. Watching her hand, Jack carefully took it from her and ate it. Mrs. Butterfield then brought the plate of cold things to Her and set them down on the table, then carried the tea tray over to follow. With a heavy sigh, Mrs. Butterfield sat down across from Her, at the end of the table. Jack came over as well, and sat next to her chair.

"Sugar?" Mrs. Butterfield asked.

She nodded.

"How many?"

She held up two fingers. Mrs. Butterfield smiled, and tossed two lumps into one of the white cups.

"Cream?"

She nodded again, and Mrs. Butterfield splashed a bit of cream in that same cup, then poured the dark, steaming tea in after it. Reaching over to take it, She gave Mrs. Butterfield a smile, making sure that the older woman saw it. She did, and returned it. And now that She could study Mrs. Butterfield closer, she found that the woman's features beamed like a warm hearth on a winter night—and her eyes sparkled.

"Of course, his manner makes him a bit intolerable to

folk who don't understand it," Mrs. Butterfield poured her own tea without cream or sugar. She chuckled. "And he's never yet met a lady who could stand his company, except his mother, his sister—oh, and Miss Harrison, the sister of one of his school friends. She only laughs at his jibes, and she listens when he discusses such complicated subjects in language and phonetics—I can barely understand whatever it is he's talking about—Oh, good heavens!" Mrs. Butterfield suddenly sat up straight. So did She, and her eyebrows raised.

"I'm just sitting here chatting with you and having tea—I've completely forgotten my manners," Mrs. Butterfield got up out of her chair and hastily dusted off her apron. "I'm afraid I've been so lonely these past months, it's made me forget my place—and here I am, presuming to speak on equal terms with a lady!"

Alarmed, She reached out and grasped Mrs. Butterfield's sleeve. Mrs. Butterfield went still, watching her...

Squeezing harder, She shook her head, and gave her another earnest smile.

"Well..." Mrs. Butterfield ventured. "As long as you don't mind..."

Again, She shook her head. And so Mrs. Butterfield sat back down. After a moment, she became comfortable once more, and began telling Her about how Basil had found the dog Jack on the street when he was just a young thing, and he had come home with Basil and become his instant friend.

28

As She listened, she carefully ate the food in front of her, and slowly drank the tea, watching the attractive dog lie down placidly between them, ears tilted toward their conversation.

After they finished, Mrs. Butterfield gathered everything up, and took it over to the counter by the large copper tank.

"Come with me, dear, and I'll set you up in a place to sleep."

So She got up and followed Mrs. Butterfield and Jack toward a door at the back of the kitchen—one that opened up into a chilly, narrow, wooden, servant's staircase. As she passed a cabinet, Mrs. Butterfield grabbed a lit lantern, and held it aloft as she started to climb.

"Keep close," Mrs. Butterfield advised. "I'll let the dog go first—he knows the way." She stepped aside and Jack clambered up the stairs and into the darkness. Then, the two women continued on.

Every step creaked with a louder and more ridiculous note. They both gathered up their skirts and treaded carefully, not wishing to trip. They wound their way up to a landing, then to another staircase. At the top of this, they stepped out onto the third floor, having skipped the second entirely. Mrs. Butterfield stepped out into this dark corridor, and spoke softly.

"This is where my rooms are, and Mr. Cutworth's. Mine are at the far end. His are here," she pointed to the shut door in front of her. "Come this way."

Together, they crept a few paces down the hall, then turned left into a little room—another library, very small. To the right and left, shelves stood floor to ceiling. An in the center of the room, an iron, spiral staircase stretched up into the next story.

Jack already perched midway up it, looking down at them. She smiled at him.

"This way." Mrs. Butterfield urged, and started up this new staircase. She followed. Finally, they rose to another landing, and Mrs. Butterfield opened the door.

"Nobody has slept in this room for about fifteen years—not since the other house maid Nelly Smith died. But I keep it in good order—I hate to have any bedroom get dusty and out of sorts."

Mrs. Butterfield went inside and took the light with her, illuminating a small, square room with a single, curtained window. A low fireplace stood empty against the far wall, and to the left of it stood an iron-framed single-sized bed wearing a white quilt and pillows, with a trunk at its foot. A red armchair waited on the other side of the fireplace, beside a little sewing table. In another corner was a vanity with a mirror, brush, comb, bowl and pitcher. Jack stood in the center of the rug, regarding Her, as if to gauge her reaction. Mrs. Butterfield quickly lit the lamp on that sewing table, then bent and swiftly started a fire, which soon started to dance and crackle.

She watched Mrs. Butterfield for a moment—and then her eye caught on something.

A brown satchel sitting on the floor near the foot of the bed.

She darted to it and snatched it up—pried open the top, looked inside—

Crushed it to her heart and closed her eyes.

"I brought that up here for you," Mrs. Butterfield said, standing up and facing her. "I knew you would be staying the night. No matter what the master said, I wasn't going to let you go out into that cold again without any rest! Especially after what happened."

All She could do was look at her, trying to smile and fighting not to cry.

"Oh, dear, it's all right," Mrs. Butterfield patted Her shoulder. "I'll go downstairs and fetch you some night clothes and a dress for tomorrow. Both Mrs. Collingwood and Miss Imogen—Mr. Collingwood's sister—leave clothes here for when they come to stay—but I'd imagine you're closer to Miss Imogen's size. Oh, and I'll get some warm water so you can have a wash. I will be right back. Come on, Jack!" And the two of them headed back down the stairs, leaving the door open, as She stood gazing after them, now warm and dry by the fire.

Chapter Three

Her footstep squeaked loudly on the first stair. She stopped and winced. Her heartbeat sped up.

She had snapped awake early that morning, just as the grey dawn filtered in through her window—and lay there for five minutes, paralyzed by disorientation. At last, when she had finally crawled up into a sitting position, breathing raggedly, she twisted around to find a fire already lit in the hearth...

And she remembered.

Swallowing, she had gathered her wits, steeled herself, pushed off the covers and slipped out onto the rug. She had then discovered a new navy-colored dress and undergarments laid out on the top of the trunk. She had also noticed that the pitcher by the basin was steaming—so she dashed away the cobwebs of her dreams, hurried over to the dresser, had a quick wash, scrubbed her teeth, dressed herself, then brushed out her hair and carefully pinned it up.

Now, she had worked her way down the spiral staircase, down the next flights to the one that re-entered the kitchen. She bit her lip, and forced herself to keep going, even as the boards made a racket of creaking and groaning.

At last, she pushed out through the door, and the scent of bread, eggs and bacon washed over her—nearly knocking her down. Her mouth instantly started to water, and her stomach growled.

"Oh, good morning, dear!" Mrs. Butterfield's voice rang through the kitchen, and She quickly found the housekeeper standing near another door, propping it open with her foot, holding a full tea tray in her hands.

"I suppose you didn't know the way—but you could have used the main staircase," Mrs. Butterfield told her, smiling. "Here, come with me, and I will get you some breakfast."

Obediently, She crossed the kitchen, and held the door open for Mrs. Butterfield.

"Thank you, dear," the housekeeper said brightly, and bustled out ahead of her into a room She had not seen before—a small breakfast room, with a square table in the center. White floral wallpaper caught the thin sunlight and brought it in, and by it showed the simple landscape paintings on the walls. The wooden floor here creaked just as loudly, and a grandfather clock in the far corner ticked sleepily right along with it.

Basil sat at the table, his back to the wall, a newspaper held up in front of him so She could see nothing of him but

33

his hands. Mrs. Butterfield set the clattering tea tray down on the table and set his breakfast in front of him.

"Here you are, Mr. Collingwood. I will be right back with yours, dear," Mrs. Butterfield told Her. "Be seated if you like." And she swept back to the kitchen.

She hesitated a moment, then slid out the chair across from Basil and sat down, bracing the edge of her corset on the wooden seat so that she sat perfectly erect.

Basil flapped the paper closed, then turned a page— and She caught the gleam of his reading spectacles. He saw her. But he didn't say anything. She gripped her fingers together under the table.

Another few moments of silence passed, and then he finally slapped the paper shut, folded it, and dropped it onto the floor. He wore a crisp, dark-grey morning suit, silk patterned waistcoat and dark tie, and his hair was combed neatly. He then took off his spectacles and set them on the tablecloth, grabbed his napkin and laid it out on his lap.

And then he lifted his icy eyes and frowned intently at her.

"It appears you stayed the night after all," he stated, glancing quickly across her whole frame. "Sleep well?"

She gauged his tone, felt only cold curiosity behind it—but nodded anyway.

"Mhm," he said, watching her, then picked up his utensils and began to cut into his bacon. The next moment, Mrs. Butterfield returned with another tray, and set out a steaming plate just as laden with eggs, bacon, potatoes and a roll, as well as a glass of milk, and tea for Her.

"You take your tea the same as Mr. Collingwood," Mrs. Butterfield remarked. "Must say, it makes it easy for me to remember!"

Basil eyed Mrs. Butterfield for an instant as he chewed, but she ignored it, and briskly headed to the kitchen again, muttering,

"Coal smut on that wallpaper again...Never know why the mistress picked that color...Never an end to the scrubbing..."

She watched Mrs. Butterfield go, and her mouth started watering again. So, taking great care, she picked up her fork and knife, cut into her own bacon, and began to eat.

Methodically, she worked her way around the plate, eating everything, taking sips equally from her milk and her tea. And she felt Basil watching her every movement— though he made no comment.

The other door nearer Basil opened, and Mr. Cutworth, looking as smart, pressed and slicked as if he were attending the queen's funeral, entered with a tray bearing letters.

"The morning mail, sir," he said, holding it out. Basil put his utensils down and took the envelopes off the tray.

"How was your evening, sir?" Mr. Cutworth asked.

"Dismal," Basil sighed, flicking through the mail. "There is a *reason* why a club for the most unsociable men in England never hosts dinner parties. The conversation was appalling. Mycroft never would have allowed such a mangled attempt at social nonsense. But, alas...I believe he's on the continent."

"Speaking of Mr. Holmes," Mr. Cutworth spoke up. "I believe there is a letter there from his brother—a young man living on Baker Street."

"Brother? I didn't know he had one," Basil frowned, turning the letter over. "'Mr. Sherlock Holmes.' Hm. Never heard of him." He stacked the letters and handed them back to Mr. Cutworth, unopened. "Put them on my desk, Cutworth. I'll get to them when I'm not busy."

"Yes, sir," Mr. Cutworth turned and left. She watched him go too, dabbing her mouth with her napkin.

"Hm," Basil said again—and when She looked at him, she saw he was already studying her. She set her napkin back down in her lap, falling into stillness as he finished his breakfast. She felt as if she were tilting on the edge of a precipice, the bottom of the pit she hovered over completely hidden from her...

Basil cleared his throat, wiped his mouth on his napkin as well, pushed back and got to his feet. She leaned back, staggered again by his intimidating height, and crushed the napkin in her grip.

"Come," he beckoned to her. "Let's see if we can't figure out what you are."

She blinked, but he just turned and left through the same door Mr. Cutworth had used, so she stood, put her napkin down, scooted her chair in and followed him.

They emerged into the same hallway she had seen last night, the one that passed the dining room presided over by Leonidas the lion. Basil charged on ahead and turned left, entering the front room. His purposeful strides *screeked* across the floor until his shoes met a rug. She trailed after, uncertain, as he made his way past the piano and to his desk. He then turned, faced her, leaned back against that desk and folded his arms.

"Come closer," he muttered, beckoning once more with his long fingers. She did so, then stood there in silence for a long moment as his gaze sliced through her. She soon found she couldn't bear to look back at him—it was like putting her hand near a flame—so she glanced around the library. She could see more of it now, since the windows behind her had been unveiled, and the morning light invaded to show her the details on the spines of the books, the glimmer of the brass on the lamps—and the facets of frost in Basil's eyes.

"Cannot speak, cannot write," Basil suddenly said into the silence, his voice deep and exact. "Yet can understand English when it's spoken. Excellent table manners, but ate far too much for a well-bred city girl of means. A girl from the country, then. Well-groomed, with hair done immaculately—and not by a maid. Middle class. Am I right?"

She stared at him, then nodded slowly.

"You have no way of telling me who you are," he pressed. "No references in that satchel of yours?"

She shook her head.

"So no one sent you."

She shook her head again.

"Wait," he held up a hand. "Are you agreeing or disagreeing with me?"

She hesitated. He groaned and shook his head.

"Are you agreeing with me, that no one sent you?"

She hesitated again, then nodded. He stood away from the desk, one arm crossed over his chest, the other raised so his finger draped over his lips.

"You have a name?"

Alarm flashed through her, and before she could help herself, she'd given him a wicked look.

"Of course you do," he muttered. "Is it common?"

She tightened her jaw, but she shrugged one shoulder.

"Mary?" he guessed.

She shook her head.

"Alice? Anna? Clara?"

She shook her head again.

"Elizabeth? Ida? No." He folded his arms again. "Not wasting my time with that. Not important, anyway. So, you can't tell me who you are. Can you tell me where you've come from?"

She fought not to let the heat show in her face, but she was sure it did. He strode around his desk, reached up and pulled down a map from a hanging roller atop the book case, so that the expanse covered the shelves. The first was a map of the world, and he jabbed a finger at the continent.

"Have you come from somewhere else in Europe?"

She shook her head.

"All right, then." He reached up and pulled another map down to cover it. "England."

Her pulse picked up, and she stepped closer, straining as she gazed at the markings on the map...

"All right, so here we are," Basil thumped his finger down. "London. Are you from London?"

She shook her head.

"Ugh, of course not. Might as well make this *really* difficult," He rubbed his eyes. "Now, have you come from the south, the west, the east, or the north?"

She wrapped her arms around her middle, grinding her teeth. He sighed and raked his hand through his hair.

"South?"

She shook her head.

"East?"

Shook her head.

"North? No. West it is, then." He began trailing his finger straight north from London. "All right, we've passed Bracknell...Maidenhead and...High Wycombe..."

She began edging closer, taking fistfuls of the sides of her dress, holding her breath...

"Reading...Newbury Woking is down there somewhere..." His finger kept wandering steadily westward. "Almost to Swindon, with Oxford to the—"

She slapped her hand down on the desk with a ringing *thud.*

He spun and stared at her.

"Oxford?" he repeated.

She nodded fiercely. He faced the map again.

"Interesting." He paused a moment, then turned to her. "Come here."

She didn't move.

"Come *here*," he ordered sharply. She wrapped her arms around herself again, feeling like giving him another wicked glare, and slowly walked around the desk and up to the map.

"How did you get here? Did you walk?"

She gave him an ugly sideways look.

"Train?" he pressed. "What stations did you use? Point to them."

She stared at him, then up at the map, suddenly feeling her hands go cold.

"Point to them," he barked. She swallowed, her breath unsteadying.

"Can't even read," he muttered darkly. "Wonderful. How in heaven's name did you manage to buy a ticket?"

She faced him and blushed so that her face hurt. His eyes narrowed.

"You sneaked your way on, didn't you? Why?"

She lifted her chin, her mouth tensing.

"What was so important about getting to London?" He crossed his arms and leveled a terrible regard down upon her. "Did you steal something? Is that what's in the satchel? Are you running from the law?"

She shook her head firmly, once. His eyes flashed.

"A man, then. Your husband?"

Again, shook her head, her cheeks burning.

"All right, your wicked father or mother," he said flippantly. "Stepfather, stepmother?"

Again and again, she shook her head.

"Do you even *have* a mother or father? Brother or sister? Guardian? Any family at all?" he demanded.

She shook her head, pain sliding down her ribs.

"No one," he stated, pinning her with his tone. "Do you own anything? Do you have a home, any possessions at all?"

She shivered, and shook her head for the last time.

And he laughed.

She gaped at him, baffled.

"Aha, I see," he crowed. "This wasn't planned at all, was it? You didn't plan to knock on *my* particular door— you could have easily just picked Mrs. Halifax across the street, couldn't you?" He pointed at her. "You've had no luck finding a husband or a situation in Oxford, so you've merrily hopped a train to London because you've heard that's where all the rich, gullible people live, and you thought you'd try your hand at getting hired by one of them—or better yet, installing yourself as an inconspicuous leech feeding off his or her good graces." He waved dismissively, turned to his desk and picked up his letters. "Well, I'm not in the market for a charity case today, but I'll certainly drop a line to Mrs. Halifax—a dumb, illiterate house maid might be just what she needs."

She picked up his glass inkwell and hurled it at the map.

It struck the hard surface and exploded.

The deafening shatter shook the house. Black ink shot all across the face of England. Glass rained onto the wood floor.

Basil leaped backward—

She turned and fled, racing up the main staircase as fast as she could, bursting onto the second floor, dashing past several closed doors and forbidding portraits until she found another staircase. Gasping, she charged up it, her vision blinking in and out, turned, and blundered into the iron spiral staircase. She hauled herself up that case, threw herself into the tower room and slammed the door.

She pulled in deep, rapid breaths, but her head spun. Shakily, she unbuttoned the front of her dress, pulled it off her arms and pushed it down around her waist, and frantically loosened the stays of her corset.

The tension in her chest instantly eased, and air flooded her lungs.

Her head cleared. She leaned forward against her bed, taking fistfuls of the quilt and closing her eyes.

Words flashed against her eyelids. Words and letters. Always words and letters, words and letters and sounds...

Her left hand ached, and twitched.

She straightened up, swiped at her eyes, and turned around, searching the room. At last, her attention landed on the trunk. She fell to her knees in front of it and threw it open...

She snatched at the pile of stationery, a bottle of ink and a pen she found inside. She dragged them out, shut the trunk, and set the paper down on top of it. With trembling fingers, she opened the bottle of ink, dipped the pen in...

Squeezed her eyes shut tightly, pressed the nib to the paper and wrote two words—the words that had burned themselves into the depths of her mind.

Harcourt Winchester

A few hours later, deep and grim wind began thudding against the walls of the tower, and soon whipped around it in low, lonely howling. A chill seeped in through the chinks in the window, forcing her to re-lace her stays—though not as tightly—and clothe herself again. With her dress buttoned, she crept toward the fire and knelt down in front of it on the rug, grasping the piece of paper on her lap. She stared down at the words she had written—but she couldn't read them. If she hadn't written them herself, she wouldn't have been able to even venture a guess.

She sighed, folded the paper, and slipped it into the pocket of her skirt. The wind groaned and wuthered, almost as it had out on the moors...

She got up, shaking loose of that thought, wandered over to the window and pushed the curtain aside.

Snow. It tumbled in grey curtains, swirling like dervishes upon the flat roof of the neighboring house just below her.

Snuff. Snuff, snuff, snuff.

She paused, then faced the door, wrapping her arms around herself.

Snuff-snuff-snuff-snuff...

The sound grew more insistent, and emanated from the bottom of the door. Frowning, she stepped up to it, her heels tapping, worked the knob and opened it.

Jack instantly lifted his head and perked his ears at her—tilted his head and brightly met her eyes. He had been sniffing her through the crack.

She smiled a little. He wagged his tail. Then, expertly, he turned on a dime and clambered loudly down the spiral staircase. She watched him go, wondering...

She heard him stop down in the little library, panting quietly.

Then, with another terrific metallic clamor, he came up the stairs toward her again. He stopped, watching her.

"Mhmf," he barked very softly at her, almost keeping his mouth shut, and wagged his tail again. He bounced once, then turned back around and went back down. This time, he kept going, and she could hear his claws clacking in the hallway.

She hesitated, then started down the stairs too, careful to take hold of the hand rail.

And then she stopped.

Quiet humming, from the far end of the hall.

The tune of "Greensleeves."

She gripped the railing and closed her eyes, letting the notes wash through her.

Then, finally, she opened her eyes, and stepped out into the hallway. Mr. Cutworth's door was shut, but she could see light and hear sounds from further down the hall. She crept into the plain corridor, following the worn carpet to the end, where she found a door ajar. Carefully, she peered inside...

Mrs. Butterfield sat in a red armchair by the fireplace. A basket of laundry sat beside her feet, and a white shirt lay spread on her lap. The room was small, but had one window that probably overlooked the street, but its panes were covered in frost. A simple bed, dresser and wash stand stood in all available space against the walls, and a rag rug covered the floor. Another chair, empty, sat opposite the housekeeper, and a small table stood between the chairs, covered in tea things and sandwiches. The housekeeper hummed to herself, peering through wire-rimmed spectacles

45

at her sewing.

Jack trotted in ahead of Her, and touched his nose to Mrs. Butterfield's elbow. Mrs. Butterfield's head came up, and she smiled at Her.

"Hello, dear! Can I get you something?"

She shook her head. Mrs. Butterfield moved to stand up.

"Would you like a bite to eat? I'll just make up something for you. I'm just doing a bit of mending—it's so much warmer in the smaller rooms. The big rooms get drafty in the wintertime."

Shaking her head insistently, She stepped forward and held out a hand. Mrs. Butterfield paused.

"All right, then." She eased back down in her chair, patted Jack on the head, then picked up her sewing. "Please come and sit, and eat what you like of this. I'm used to taking a luncheon, as Mrs. Collingwood and Miss Collingwood always enjoyed it, and still do when they come—and it helps me keep up my strength. Mr. Basil usually has breakfast here, then studies until perhaps two, and then he goes out to tea—only ever the same tea shop, down on the corner. And if he has supper here, it is usually at about seven o'clock. But he's gone out today—I'm sure I don't know where. Said he wouldn't be back until evening time. I'm glad he didn't take Jack along with him."

Watching Mrs. Butterfield's steady hands, She sat down across from her and poured herself some tea, with sugar and cream, and picked up a few sandwiches onto a plate.

"Mr. Cutworth has gone running errands for me. Stout man, in this weather," Mrs. Butterfield remarked. "Hope he doesn't catch cold. I've sent him to get ham hocks and flour and sugar and butter. I mean to do some baking tomorrow. That ought to warm up the house..."

She listened, drank her tea and painstakingly ate her sandwiches as Mrs. Butterfield talked more about the household chores, and her favorite recipes, whilst Jack lay down on the rug between them, drowsily glancing back and forth. The fire crackled in accompaniment with Mrs. Butterfield's narrative, until She had finished her meal.

"Do you knit, dear?"

Her head came up, and she blinked.

Then, slowly, she nodded.

"You do? Would you like some yarn to try?" Mrs. Butterfield asked. "I have some beautiful red here...Ah, yes," she bent over the side of her chair and pulled out a ball of blazing scarlet yarn from a basket, and two long needles. She leaned forward and handed them to Her. Carefully, She took them.

"A very soft yarn, that," Mrs. Butterfield told her. "Good for making scarves. And knitting is perfect for this bleak weather, isn't it?"

Absently, She nodded again, feeling the yarn, slowly pulling a strand of it loose from the ball, as remembrance sparked through her fingertips...

Then, before she knew it, she had cast on—fifteen

loops, exactly—and had knitted her first line.

Fire ignited in her heart, and strength filled her hands. She looked up at Mrs. Butterfield, met her eyes—and grinned.

"What a beautiful smile you have!" Mrs. Butterfield cried. "Really, such a lovely young lady." Her warm expression filled with sharp sympathy. "I really cannot tell you how thankful I am that you are sitting here, with me, beside this fire, instead of out there in that dreadful fog and snow."

She nodded in reply, earnestly. Jack's tail thumped against the rug.

Then, an eager fever in her fingers, She picked up the knitting, and swiftly set to work.

Chapter Four

The moment the little clock on the mantel struck 4 o'clock, Mrs. Butterfield got up from her chair, and begged Her pardon, but she had to go polish the brasses and clean the kitchen. Mrs. Butterfield said She was welcome to remain in her room as long as she liked to finish her knitting. Then, she and Jack left, and headed down the stairs.

Sighing, She gazed down at her half-finished scarf as the room fell silent, save for the crackling fire. She sat back in her chair, tiredly took it back up and worked it about half an hour longer, until her fingers started to ache. Finally, she got to her feet and set her work on the seat of the chair, then ventured out into the hallway.

That instant, she glimpsed Mr. Cutworth emerge from his room and briskly shut the door—She ducked back into the doorway so he wouldn't see her. She listened as his footsteps crossed the hallway and descended the stairs before she edged out, and wandered toward the same end of the hallway...

She paused before the wide staircase next to the little library—the staircase that would lead to the "main" staircase, as Mrs. Butterfield had called it. She bit her lip, and glanced toward the servants' staircase...

And decided she would rather not run into Mr. Cutworth in such a confined space.

So, as quietly as she could, she started down the stairs, sliding her hand along the polished bannister. These stairs were not carpeted, but still made of fine wood, and rather wide. White plaster walls, with no adornment at all. However, though they were not dusty, these stairs did not squeak.

She arrived at a landing where she found a beautiful oak door with brass handle—doubtlessly the door to the family bedrooms. She gazed at it a moment, listening, then turned and started down to the next level...

Stopped, and gazed.

Thick scarlet carpet cascaded down the steps. Lavish red wallpaper decorated with a gold floral pattern graced the whole of the towering stairwell. Lamps accompanied the grand portraits presiding over everyone who dared to pass this way.

She wandered down, keeping her hand on the bannister, studying each face and feature held within the luxurious golden frames.

All ages of people—husbands, wives and children—

dressed finely and conservatively, in dress styles ranging from the plain, high-collared black of the 1860's to the frills, ruffles and wigs of the early 18th century. She reached the landing, and paused before a large portrait of a serious, handsome family standing before a fireplace. A tall, stately man with dark eyes, dark hair and a beard; a woman his age with gold curls and vivid blue eyes; a girl that looked exactly like a younger version of her mother—but with mischief sparkling in her emerald gaze and touching the edge of her pretty mouth; and a boy next to her, with curly brown hair—and a gaze like summer lightning.

She put a hand to her chest.

Basil.

This was his family.

For a long time, she stood there, studying each of them. Deep smile lines marked the father's features. Sharp intelligence marked his wife's. But Basil looked as if he had not smiled for the entirety of his childhood.

She turned and descended the rest of the staircase, feeling warmth rise up to greet her. She stepped off the last one—

The floor board beneath her foot *squeaked.*

She froze. Her gaze darted over to the door...

Nothing.

She could hear Mrs. Butterfield in the kitchen, but that lady hummed away and clattered with the pans. Nobody came into the parlor.

Fire spat and muttered in the hearth. The lamps on the

walls flickered. She meandered deeper into the library, attention flickering across the spines of the hundreds and hundreds of books...

She almost reached out and touched the piano keys— then pulled her hand back.

A clock on the mantel ticked dully and steadily. Mrs. Butterfield kept humming in the depths of the house— some cheerful country milking tune.

At last, She screwed up her courage, stretched out her hand, and set her fingertips on the spine of a small, thin red book the size of a novel. Biting her lip, she glanced over her shoulder at the door again...

No one.

So she pulled it down.

Frowning hard, she held it there in both hands for a long while, then cautiously opened the front cover.

Words. Words on the front page.

She stared at them. Closed her eyes tightly. Opened them again, and stared.

Furiously turned a page. More words.

More nonsensical words.

She slapped the book shut, covering her face with her hand, and fought to calm her breathing.

Finally, she shoved the book back onto the shelf and turned away from all the books, folding her arms.

She stepped into the parlor section, onto the rug in front of the fireplace, and made herself attend to all the baubles and knick-knacks packed onto the mantel instead.

However, true curiosity suddenly caught her, and she peered closer.

Porcelain figurines of French courtiers; lacquered Chinese boxes; jade Buddhas, ivory elephants; glimmering golden Russian icons, American Indian beadwork upon small pieces of leather; wooden heads making terrifying faces; little square paintings of the canals in Venice...

And above this treasure trove—

She blinked.

An oval portrait behind curved glass. A portrait of a cherubic little boy—wheat-colored curls; bright, large blue eyes, and a ready smile. He looked about eight years old. He wore a tidy sailor suit, and a crooked hat.

The portrait was covered in dust.

For a long while, she stood, wondering at this—and glancing back up the stairs toward the large portrait of the family.

A sound outside. The clap of hooves—the clatter of wheels.

She turned toward the window.

Voices. The snort of a horse.

She ventured closer, pushed the curtains out of the way, and rubbed the frost loose so she could see.

A hansom outside, parked in front of the house just next door—the house upon whose roof she could gaze from her tower window. A finely-dressed woman with a large hat and thick coat stepped down out of the hansom, and immediately turned around to lift a little child out with her.

He wore a brown suit and coat, and a flat hat pulled down around his ears. She set him down on the cobbles, said a brisk word to the driver, then quickly grabbed the little boy's hand and pulled him after her toward the house, ducking against the wind and gusting snow.

She watched the pair climb the stairs and enter the house. Slowly, She sank down onto the window seat, keeping the curtain back so she could see out, watching the Londoners hustle past her, dipping their heads and holding their collars.

But every once in a while, her gaze was inexplicably drawn back to the treasures on the mantel—and the cheerful face of the little boy all shrouded in dust.

She sighed, gazing up at the shadows on the ceiling, her fingers interlaced and her hands resting on her chest. She lay on her bed, still wearing her day dress, listening to the crackle of the low fire.

Just a while ago, she had heard several clocks down below in the house chime. She had closed her eyes, and counted...

...7...8...9...10...11...12.

The wind kept moaning around the tower, occasionally gusting down the chimney. She had closed the drapes to combat the chill, yet it still seeped in. She ought to get into her night clothes and crawl underneath these thick blankets...

A tune wandered through her head. A tune that, long ago, had always accompanied needlework of any kind...by a plain fireplace...surrounded by a dozen other girls in black dresses, aprons and white caps...

She sat up, her chest tightening. She got to her feet, pressing her icy hands together, then moved to the door and opened it.

Cold washed over her. She shivered and rubbed her arms, but took the plunge anyway.

She climbed down the metal staircase as quietly as she could, entered the hallway and turned right, then proceeded down the servant's staircase until she pushed out into the dark kitchen.

A low light rose from the embers of the range fire. She paused a moment to let her eyes adjust, then crept through, her shoes tapping again, and walked into the hallway with the portraits. She passed the dining room—hardly visible at all in the blackness—and found her way into the front library.

A bit more of a fire burned there, tossing ghostly shadows across the faces of the shelves. She hesitated, holding her breath, listening...

But she heard nothing but silence, and the deep moaning of the winter wind against the walls of the house.

She relaxed her chest, feeling the warmth of this room

creep into her arms and feet, and her gaze landed on the book-covered piano. A pang traveled through her.

She hesitated, then stole toward it. Reaching out, She ran her fingers across the smooth side of the wooden instrument, and edged around to the keyboard.

She gazed down at the black and white keys, then cautiously sat down at the bench. She laid her hands upon the keys, then glanced up at the ceiling and bit her lip.

Surely, if she played quietly, the roar of the storm would drown her out, and wouldn't disturb anyone.

Drawing in another deep breath, She began to play, very softly, a tune she'd known since she was a little girl. Slow...Wistful...Old.

The piano's notes resonated down into the floor, and filled the silent room. As she played, her hands filled with strength, and images flooded her head. She closed her eyes and felt her way across the keyboard, relishing the sensation of the vibration of the song travelling through her body as she worked the pedal. The melody and harmony swept around her, the frosty storm fading to the background. She took a deep breath...

And began to hum.

She hummed the sad, longing melody—it pulled through her chest, her voice relaxing with a gentle vibrato, resonating through her head. Memories swam through her mind—faded and golden with age, like old photographs.

A little room, hidden from the wuthering wind, crowded with girls. A young woman sitting on a short chair next to the fire, her brilliant red curls tucked under her cap in a vain effort to contain them. Her kind, vivid blue eyes, framed by a myriad of freckles, glancing out at her little charges as she sang like a thrush, and worked her needle swiftly up and down, up and down...

Still humming, She got lost in the notes, transported by their echoes. The words meandered across her eyelids, but she kept her lips closed. The song swelled to its crescendo, and she finished it out, her fingers lingering on the last chord.

"Ar Eirinn Ni Neosfainn Ce Hi, is it not?"

She jumped terribly, her eyes opening. She jerked her hands off the keyboard. Frantically, she searched the shadows of the room for whoever had spoken...

Movement from the chair by the fireplace—the chair with its back to her.

Basil Collingwood slowly stood up from that chair, buttoned his coat, and turned around to look at her. Half in firelight, half black as ink, his sharp, cutting silhouette stood tall and imperial; his brow frowning, his gaze as intent as winter midnight.

He had been there the entire time.

Her heart slammed against her breastbone and took off—the heat drained out of her head.

Deliberately, he clasped his hands behind his back.

"An Irish tune," he mused, his voice a low rumble of thunder. "Translates to 'For Ireland, I'll Not Say Her Name.' Am I right?"

She didn't move.

He ducked his head. Then he turned, and gazed behind him into the fire.

She couldn't tear her attention from him. She could see edges of sapphire in his eyes now, in profile—the deepening furrow of his brow as his gaze distanced.

She held her breath. Her pulse deafened her, and sent painful throbs to the ends of her fingers...

Then, suddenly, he took a breath and faced her.

"I will help you."

She blinked. Stared. Her lips parted.

"You've come to Pendywick Place for assistance with your impediment," he said crisply. "And I will do what I can. Without a fee. I won't even require you to replace my map. However—I have one condition."

Her mouth closed. She frowned, waiting. He lifted his chin.

"You will remain here as long as I wish and allow me to study your disorder—diagnose it and document my findings and write either an article or a book about it, depending upon how complicated your defect and rehabilitation."

She jerked again at that last word, her heart skipping a beat.

"In addition, I will provide you with food and clothing—since you clearly cannot afford it—in exchange for your full and complete cooperation and submission to my study methods," he stated. "Are we agreed?"

She still stared at him, squeezing the front of her skirt. Paper crinkled beneath the fabric. She swallowed hard. And shook her head.

His frown flashed like lightning—

But confusion shot through his expression. And she leaped at the sight of it.

She jumped off of the piano stool, and stuffed her hand in her pocket. She pulled out the piece of paper, strode toward him—fighting back a shiver—and held it out.

His gaze raced over her features, penetrating her eyes, and then he took the paper from her. Turning toward the fire, he opened the folded sheet, and peered at the writing.

He froze.

Stared, transfixed. Then, slowly, he lifted his head just an inch, and looked at her.

"Did you write this?"

She nodded once.

"How?" he demanded. She stood there helplessly for a moment, almost shrugging...

Then reached up and covered her eyes with her right hand, and made the motion of writing with her left.

When she lowered her hand, and looked at him again...

He was gazing down at her as if he'd never seen anything like her on earth.

"Indeed," he whispered.

She stayed frozen, buried under his scrutiny, until he turned back to the paper.

"Harcourt Winchester. He was one of my old

professors at Oxford," he said, meeting her gaze again. "Why have you given me his name?"

Her heart leaped. She took half a step forward, her mind flying—

She pointed to her eyes, then pointed at the paper. She repeated the motion three times, then clamped her fingers together and locked her jaw, waiting.

"You need to see him," Basil guessed.

She almost jumped into the air. She nodded hard, over and over.

"You need me to take you to him," he concluded.

Again, She nodded. And again, he considered the paper.

Then, slowly, he folded it, drew himself up, faced her and clasped his hands behind his back.

"Very well. My offer still stands. I will take you to Professor Winchester if you will allow me to diagnose and study your defect."

A tremor ran through her, but she made herself look up at him. His features betrayed nothing. Finally, she nodded.

"All right, that's settled," he said crisply, suddenly turning and heading toward the door. "We'll go to Oxford on Sunday."

Panic grabbed her, and she took two steps toward him. He glanced over at her.

"That's the soonest I can possibly leave town," he said. "Tomorrow I have several patients stopping by and I cannot reschedule their appointments. It would be immensely rude." He stuffed the piece of paper in his pocket. "Get some rest. And if you have a mind to, you should get up early and help Mrs. Butterfield with breakfast. She's been short-handed since her daughter left and I know she would appreciate the assistance." He gave her a brief, insincere smile, then vanished into the dark hallway, leaving Her standing there, stunned.

But as the image of a train steaming toward Oxford, with her aboard, stormed through her mind...

She set her jaw, fire burning in her heart, and squeezed her hands into fists.

Chapter Five

A clattering, deep in the house, shook her dreams loose.

"All right girls, wake up. Make your beds, wash your faces, get dressed. I want everything neat and orderly in this room. No exceptions, no dawdling. You have ten minutes. The last girl to fall in line will do without breakfast."

She twitched, her fingers clamping down on the blankets, and opened her eyes. Glimpsed the low fire in the hearth. Shivered. The sharp female voice faded into silence.

Stiffly, she turned over and glanced at the window. Dawn soaked in through the curtains. Drawing a deep breath, then letting it out slowly, she calmed her heartbeat and remembered where she was.

Then, she pushed the covers off, got up, had a wash, dressed, pinned up her hair and made her bed, then headed downstairs to the kitchen.

She could feel the warmth radiating up toward her through the stairwell, and hurried her pace, anxious to thaw her freezing fingers...

When She pushed the door open, the clattering of claws greeted her, and she found Jack waiting just inside, ears up, tail wagging. She smiled, bent down and petted him.

"What are *you* doing awake this early, Miss?" Mrs. Butterfield, kneeling in front of the range, cried.

Straightening, She smiled at her also, then swept a hand across the room, raising her eyebrows earnestly...

Mrs. Butterfield frowned at her, laboriously pushing herself to her feet and dusting her hands off on her apron.

"Would you like breakfast? It will take me a while, but I can make tea for you while you wait for it."

Quickly, She shook her head, stepping forward, and pointed to the range again. Then, she made stirring motions, pouring motions, and scrubbing motions, while Mrs. Butterfield watched intently.

Then, her features lit up with understanding.

"Oh, you would like to *help?*"

In answer, She nodded rapidly, taking another step forward.

"Erm...all right, then." Mrs. Butterfield rubbed her hands on her apron again, her brow furrowing. "I'll set you to work making the bacon. Think you can manage?"

Again, She nodded—and Mrs. Butterfield sprang into action. She pulled out an extra apron for Her, and then got the raw, salted bacon and skillet. At first, she gave elementary instructions—until she saw Her perform each task perfectly just as she explained. After a few remarks of awe and appreciation, she left Her alone, only tossing out remarks about where to find this or that. And then, quite quickly, the two women fell into a working rhythm, and Mrs. Butterfield merrily returned to telling stories about her childhood in Brighton, while She smiled to herself in secret satisfaction, finished the bacon, and moved on to the eggs.

She ended up eating breakfast alone—with Jack lying beside her. She listened to the ancient grandfather clock tick-tick-tick, and sneaked Jack her bread crusts under the table.

At exactly 8:30, Mrs. Butterfield came in and took Her plates away—and just as she was about to re-enter the kitchen, she turned back.

"You might enjoy sitting in on the lessons today, Miss," she said. "You could curl up in the chair in the corner while his patients come in."

Her eyes went wide. Mrs. Butterfield nodded.

"I understand—but if you could see your way to do it, it would be a great help to me. Otherwise, I will need to be there, dusting the study, and I really ought to scrub the range instead." Mrs. Butterfield adjusted the way she was holding the plates. "Mr. Collingwood prefers to have someone else present when he tutors his lady patients, you see."

Slowly, She nodded—then met Mrs. Butterfield's eyes and nodded again.

"You'd like to sit in, then?" Mrs. Butterfield asked brightly.

Again, She nodded.

"Ah, thank you, dear," Mrs. Butterfield smiled. "It's a weight off my mind, make no mistake." And she turned and bustled back into the kitchen.

In the silence, She sat there, considering the door that led to the hallway. Then, she glanced down—and realized that Jack was staring up at her, watching.

She snorted, shook her head, got to her feet and picked up her still-full teacup and saucer, and made her way through the door, Jack on her heels.

She moved down the hallway, glancing into the dining room at Leonidas, then creeping toward the front library parlor.

She hesitated at the threshold, leaning around to peer in...

Jack pushed past her skirts and trotted into the room, straight toward the parlor chairs, which had been moved slightly to face each other, with a small table in between. Basil sat in one of them—Jack went right up to the side of his chair and sat down. Absently, Basil—wearing a black suit, green waistcoat and tie, with his dark hair combed—put his hand on Jack's head, never taking his attention from the person sitting opposite him.

A woman. A young woman wearing a starched black

dress and a hat that had been fine many years ago; she had plain features, large watery brown eyes with dark circles, and a worried brow. She clutched a purse in her lap, and sat upon the edge of her chair, her lower lip trembling.

For half a minute, Basil gazed at her acutely, fingers of his left hand draped over his lips, his elbow on the armrest. Finally, he lowered his arm and folded his hands in his lap.

"So tell me about your holiday to Bath, Miss Smith," he said.

"Well, Mother and I, we went to Bath, as you said, and we started out in the morning, since the weather was fine, even though Mr. Bakehurst had forgotten to light the fires in the parlor and the kitchens," Miss Smith began, twisting the purse in her fingers. "And we rode out by the...I forget which park, the birds there are red and black, the dog came with us, and I had my favorite dress, but not my scarf, and the coat I wanted had a hole in the sleeve, and Mother brought the mending, but in the carriage, you know—"

"Wait a moment, Martha," Basil interrupted. "Take a moment and breathe deeply."

Miss Smith tightly closed her mouth, and took an audible breath through her nose.

"Now," Basil said. "Tell me about the fine morning. Just the fine morning."

Still hesitating on the threshold, She frowned, listening intently, and started to edge inside.

A floorboard creaked under her shoe.

Basil did not move his head—but his glance flashed

over and found her. It flitted up and down her form—he blinked, and turned back to Miss Smith.

Swallowing, She found Miss Smith—but Miss Smith hadn't looked over at her at all. Feeling herself fade out of their attention, She sneaked further in, found a small chair in the corner by the staircase, and sat silently down in it.

"The fine day, Miss Smith," Basil prompted.

"Oh, yes, the fine day," Miss Smith re-gathered herself.

"What made it a fine day?" Basil asked.

"Well, the sun was shining, of course, and I could open a window a bit and it wasn't too cold. Mother said it was unseasonable for this time of year, for it to be so warm, but since Mr. Bakehurst so often forgets the fire, and I hadn't packed yet—"

"Wait, wait, wait," Basil cut in. "So it was a fine day, because the sun was shining, and it was warm enough to open your window."

Miss Smith thought a moment, then nodded.

"Yes."

"And then you got in the carriage, and drove by the park," Basil said. "Tell me about what you saw through your window in the park. And between each thing you tell me about, I want you to stop, and take a small breath. All right?"

Miss Smith's brow wrinkled with concern, but she nodded again.

"I saw a big stone arch...I saw a statue on top of it of an angel...I saw a man walking his dog..." she began, obediently taking a tight breath between each. "It was a terrier, it looked like. He had a dark suit and a bowler hat, the kind my father has, his club gives parties sometimes, and his red tie doesn't—"

"Wait, wait," Basil held up his fingers. "Not your father's tie. We're in the park, remember. Tell me about the park."

"Oh, yes," Miss Smith squeezed the purse. "I'm sorry, I am...I'm trying..."

"You're doing very well today," Basil said. "Tell me what you saw after you saw the man walking his dog."

Until a quarter to ten, Miss Smith narrated her tale of her trip to Bath, often bumbling off into other subjects and down rabbit trails, her sentences cluttering together—but always, Basil called her back, reminding her to take breaths, to pause, to stay within the appropriate line of conversation. Never once did he lose patience, or even speak sharply to her. Calm and precise, he watched her and listened to her with the coolness of a reptile.

When Miss Smith left, Mrs. Butterfield trundled in with a tea tray, and set it on the small table by Basil. She smiled at Her as she passed by to return to the kitchen—and a few minutes later she came back with a little rolling trolley laden with another small tea set and tarts, and she stopped it by Her chair.

"Thought you might like a bite," Mrs. Butterfield winked at Her. Smiling brightly, She sat up and squeezed Mrs. Butterfield's wrist—and Mrs. Butterfield patted her hand. The next moment, the bell rang, and Mrs. Butterfield went to the door to admit the next patient.

An older woman, perhaps seventy years old, wearing black also, and a cap, sat in a fine, rattling wheelchair pushed by a young, handsome, extremely well-dressed man in a top hat. The lady had a large hooked nose; small, pinched eyes, severe mouth, and grey coloring. Her escort looked ruddy, with bright blue eyes, dark hair and a ready smile.

"Hello, good morning, Mrs. Butterfield," he said cheerfully as he pushed the lady on through and into the parlor. "How are you today?"

"Very well, Lord Brody, thank you," Mrs. Butterfield replied, closing the door after him.

"Good morning Lady Brody; Fred," Basil greeted them, rising to his feet and holding out his hand to shake Fred's.

"Good morning, Basil, old chap," Fred grinned at him, shaking his hand vigorously. "Hullo, Jack!" Fred bent to tousle the dog's ears as Jack panted happily. And then the old lady said something.

In the midst of pouring her tea, She paused—and her head came up, and she stared at the old woman, baffled at the sound she made.

Garbled and completely unintelligible—as if the poor lady had marbles in her mouth. She gestured to Basil, and then at the window, rather emphatically.

Quickly stopping her tea just before it overflowed, She set her teapot down and watched for the two men's reactions.

Fred smiled weakly—but Basil clasped his hands behind his back and gave the lady a frank look.

"Indeed, the weather really is quite ghastly. You're a soldier, Lady Brody, to brave it this particular morning."

The lady gave another garbled reply, and patted Fred's hand.

"Would you care for some tea?" Basil asked, gesturing to it. Again, the lady mumbled something, and nodded.

"I'll be off, then," Fred said, extending his hand to Basil. "I'm back to collect her at half eleven."

"Of course, see you then," Basil said, shaking his hand once more. Fred then turned to leave—

And caught sight of Her sitting there, about to take a sip of tea.

She froze. So did he.

Fred's blue eyes warmed, and he smiled at her. Her heart skipped a beat.

"Forgive me, Basil—I don't believe I'm acquainted with this young lady," he said.

"Oh, her," Basil sighed. "She's another patient of mine."

"A patient!" Fred said in surprise. "Surely not." He turned his grin back to her. "She's far too lovely to be in need of any of *your* fuss."

She blushed, and swallowed.

"Oh, nonsense," Basil said, sitting back down in his chair. "There isn't anything *less* relevant to the acquiring or possession of a speech impediment than *loveliness*."

"Well, introduce us then, old man!" Fred urged. "You're being quite rude."

"I can't," Basil answered flatly, pouring the tea. "She's stone dumb. I have no idea what her name is, nor does anybody else."

"Good lord," Fred cried, turning to Her in shock.

She blushed again, painfully...

But his smile returned, and he leaned toward her.

"It truly is unfortunate, I must say, but I look forward to talking with you some other day," he said kindly, in sotto voce. "Basil here's the best I've ever heard of, mark my words, and if anyone can cure you, it'll be him." He straightened up. "So I shall leave you with my name—Lord Fredrick Brody—and I eagerly await the day when you'll do me the honor of giving me yours."

She smiled at him, her cheeks still hot, and dipped her head.

"Get out of here, Brody, and check the *Times* for the boxing scores," Basil ordered carelessly. "It's your fault I'm neglecting your mother."

The old lady barked an equally-brusque admonition to her son, though She had no idea what she said. Covering her mouth with her hand, She stifled a laugh—and Fred winked at her.

"Good day," Fred bid them, crisply putting his top hat back on and striding toward the door. "I'll be back soon, Mother!" and with a gust of wintry air, he was gone, and

She turned her attention back to the new guest.

However, this meeting ran entirely differently from the one before. This time Basil said next to nothing, except an occasional "Indeed," or "Hm," or "Yes, of course," as the old lady mumbled and slurred between sips of tea and bites of tart. Basil also ate, very methodically, and rarely took his eyes from the old lady—attending to her with a line between his eyebrows. Jack got up from Basil's side and sat down next to Lady Brody, and often, the old woman would lower a palsied hand, and pat him on the head.

At fifteen minutes to noon, Fred returned, and with a great bustle and noise—and another merry greeting thrown in Her direction—Fred wheeled his mother back out into the winter day.

As Mrs. Butterfield shut the door in their wake and hurried over to take the tea tray away from the table near Basil, he sighed, sat back in his chair and rubbed his brow.

"Headache, sir?" Mrs. Butterfield asked in concern. "I can make up a cold compress for you, as your next appointment isn't until half past one."

"No, I don't have a headache, but I'm certain she has," Basil muttered dropping his hand—then gesturing to the space where Lady Brody had just been. Mrs. Butterfield paused and frowned.

"What do you mean, if I may ask, sir?"

Basil looked up at her, frank and open—with a tinge of weariness.

"She has a growth on her brain. I'm certain of it," he

72

said. "Did you not see her forehead? Clearly deformed, and quite different than she looked a year or so ago when she was still walking." He sighed again, shaking his head, his gaze growing distant. "The signs are all there: slurred speech, paralysis, pupil dilation in one eye…I've told Fred, and he seemed concerned enough—promised he would tell his older brother. But it seems…" he arched one eyebrow. "Since I'm not a *medical doctor*, my advice has been…ignored."

"That can't be Lord Fred's doing, surely," Mrs. Butterfield said. "He's always esteemed you so highly, even when you were at school together."

"I'm certain Fred informed Robert of my recommendation," Basil stared into the fire. "Just as I'm fairly certain, by the fact that they are still paying me for *speech* treatments, that Robert told him I have no idea what I'm talking about."

"Ooh, that Lord Robert," Mrs. Butterfield fumed, starting toward the kitchen with her clinking tea tray. "I'd give him a piece of my mind if I could—to let his poor mother suffer like that…" and she disappeared into the hallway.

For a moment, She watched the place where she'd gone, then turned back to consider Basil.

Basil sat motionless for several minutes. Then—

"Mr. Cutworth," he barked. She jumped.

Hurried footsteps sounded in the hallway, and the butler emerged, a little flustered—but he snapped to attention. She had almost completely forgotten about him.

"Yes, sir?"

"I'll have my coat and hat, and the leash," Basil said, standing up and buttoning his jacket. "I'm taking Jack out. Inform Mrs. Butterfield that I will take a small luncheon at one o'clock."

"Yes, sir, right away, sir," Mr. Cutworth said—and suddenly threw Her a sideways frown as he departed. She bit her lip.

Jack immediately got up and started springing around Basil's legs, tail wagging wildly, making a racket on the wooden floor.

"Yes, yes, yes, calm down," Basil muttered, moving to the door, just as Mr. Cutworth emerged with Basil's coat and scarf over his arm, and the leash, gloves and hat in the other hand.

"Thank you," Basil said as he put on his coat, scarf, hat and gloves, and put the leash on the dog. "We will be back shortly."

"Yes, sir," Mr. Cutworth answered, and Basil and Jack strode briskly out the door.

As soon as it shut, Mr. Cutworth turned and leveled a terrible scowl at Her.

She stopped moving, stunned.

"I'll have you know," Mr. Cutworth growled. "That I spent three hours scrubbing ink off of the floor and the rug where you smashed the master's inkwell. Haven't you any decency? Or do you come from a land of savages where things like *manners* are completely foreign?" He lifted his chin. "You're no mistress of mine. Mind you clean up after yourself *henceforth*." And he lifted his chin and swept out of the room.

In Basil's absence, She went into the kitchen and, with a little instruction from Mrs. Butterfield, made up cold sandwiches for the luncheon while Mrs. Butterfield completed the messy task of scrubbing the range. Mrs. Butterfield then took her upstairs to her own floor and showed her the seemingly-magical operation of the water closet and told Her that she was free to use it anytime she liked.

She then helped tidy the kitchen, and heard Basil come back home, but she did not go out when Mrs. Butterfield carried Basil's luncheon tray to him. Instead, she ate with Mrs. Butterfield in the kitchen, and didn't venture out until 1:30. But when she did, she couldn't help it—she was pulled by something deep in her chest.

The next patient turned out to be a young man named Art Singleton—a young, skinny, awkward man with ginger hair, a thousand freckles, wearing a worn, pressed black suit. She was certain he worked for an undertaker. He sat there with Basil for an hour and a half—and he stammered very painfully. However, just as with Miss Smith, Basil conversed with him coolly, without a hint of impatience. He urged Mr. Singleton to take deep breaths and regulate his breathing, to relax his sitting posture, to speak more slowly, to start over if his speech locked—to begin the difficult word with an uttered vowel instead of a consonant. Basil also engaged him in subjects which appeared to interest him, such as his family, the public dance coming up, and the young lady he would like to court. Often, Mr. Singleton's gaze darted over to find Her as she sat in her corner, but Basil always called his attention back. Jack lounged on the rug next to Basil's chair and napped.

After Mr. Singleton left, Basil sat in his chair and scribbled in a notebook for quite some time. Mrs. Butterfield came in and tended to the fires—and then brought out a tray bearing plate of sugar-drenched Turkish Delight, and a glass of milk.

Frowning, She watched the progress of this treat, wondering at it. Then, a rap came at the door. Tentative— three knocks.

Jack sat up and stared at the door, all attention.

Basil set the notebook aside, got to his feet and swiftly answered the door himself. Opened the inner door, strode out and opened the outer door. Though She straightened and strained, she could not see the newcomer.

"Hello, Peter," Basil greeted him. "Come inside out of the snow."

And then—small feet. And the bobbing of a little head

that She could just glimpse through the glass of the inside door.

Then, Basil opened that door and allowed a child inside, no more than five years old. He had big brown eyes, gold hair she could see beneath his cap, and he wore a tweed suit. He pulled off his gloves and scarf as he entered, and handed them to Basil, who took them as if this was customary. But then the little boy stopped, and stared at Her.

"Peter, this is another patient of mine," Basil said slowly. "I don't know her name because she can't tell me— her trouble is quite a bit worse than yours."

Peter smiled at her, and then waved shyly. She shifted forward in her seat, and held out her hand. He stepped forward and gripped her fingers gently.

"Good lad," Basil said quietly—and She risked a glance up at him.

For a moment, Basil looked back at her, his eyes brilliant...

Then Jack came clacking happily up, and Peter turned and, beaming, petted him effusively.

Basil swept around Peter, tossed the boy's things onto a footstool and took his seat by the fire, briskly crossing one knee over the other and slapping his hands down on the armrests.

"You'd better come eat your sweeties, Peter, before I steal them."

Peter giggled and broke into a run, and hopped up on

the chair opposite Basil, and sat on his knees. Jack trotted after him and planted himself by Peter's chair, watching his every move.

"Take off your hat first, Mr. Manners," Basil warned. Peter swiped it off his head with a grin and put it on his lap, then carefully picked up a cube of Turkish Delight with two fingers and ate it.

"Now, tell me about school this week," Basil prompted. And Peter spoke around his mouthful.

She couldn't understand him very well, though she could pick out about half his words. His sounds were malformed, and even when he didn't have Turkish Delight in his mouth, the muscles of his lips and tongue seemed weak. He avidly told Basil a myriad things, however, and Basil engaged him with great and eager interest—leaning forward, even chuckling—as if this was the first person in months that he actually *wanted* to talk to. Basil's features, his aspect, changed entirely—became avid and bright. She didn't recognize him—and she couldn't tear her eyes from him.

After Peter's storytelling concluded, and the Turkish Delight and milk had vanished, Peter wiped his mouth and sat on the chair properly, his feet dangling over the edge. Basil then moved the table out of the way, shifted his own chair closer, and leaned toward the little boy, bracing his elbows on his knees.

"All right, Peter, we're going to practice a bit, all right?"

Peter nodded.

"I want you to watch me carefully, and say exactly as I say."

Peter nodded again.

From thence, Basil began saying a series of phrases, such as "My mother goes to the market," "The dog walks with my father," "Cook bakes on Wednesdays," and "I will win the chess match," very slowly and deliberately. After each phrase, Peter endeavored to repeat what Basil had just said. Some, he completed with relative ease, with only a few distortions. Others caused him a great deal of difficulty, especially the combination of the words "chess match." If Peter had trouble, Basil broke the phrase into pieces, speaking only one or two words, and having Peter say them back. With remarkable precision, Basil worked him through half an hour of exercises, and Peter, though he occasionally fidgeted, attended to Basil very well, and eventually succeeded in speaking each phrase intelligibly.

At last, the clock struck half past three, and Basil got up.

"Well done, my lad," he said. "Put on your things, I'll walk you next door."

It was then that She suddenly recognized him—the little boy the lady had lifted out of the carriage yesterday in the snowstorm.

"Mr. Cutworth," Basil called again, and the butler emerged once more, looking a little haggard, with a smear of boot polish on his forehead. Basil sighed.

"I'll get my coat myself if you are going to get polish all over it."

"Oh! So sorry, sir!" Mr. Cutworth blanched, and dashed away. Soon, he returned, only a red mark on his forehead betraying the fact that he'd wiped the polish off, carrying Basil's things.

"I am walking Peter back to his mother's house," Basil told him, donning his coat and hat. "After that, I'm going to the library, then to dine at the Rules. I'll have tea at ten. Tell Mrs. Butterfield."

"Yes, sir."

"Come along, Peter," Basil motioned to him, and together the towering philologist and the little boy left Pendywick Place, while She sat alone in her tea corner, pondering everything she had just seen.

Chapter Six

She flew into a sitting position, thrashing violently—

Pain crashing through her head, blood running into her eyes, down her chin, onto her dress—a terrible *thud-thud-thud* as she tumbled down a hill, whipped by dead grass, pelted by rocks and sand, torn by briar and vine—

She forced her eyes open, gasps tearing through her chest. She frantically slapped her hands to her face, her throat her chest, feeling for the hot, sticky blood in her hair, on her face...

No.

Cold sweat and clammy skin met her shaking fingers—but no syrupy blood. She looked down. She wore a white nightgown, not a dress. And it was clean. So were the bedsheets.

Bed sheets?

She locked her jaw, reining in her terrified breathing, and squeezed the comforter hard in both hands. Sweat trickled down her temples as she blinked, over and over, clearing the vivid, horrid memories from her mind, replacing them with the image of the window in front of her, through which feeble, wintery daylight peered.

The window of the tower room at Pendywick Place.

London. Mrs. Butterfield. Jack.

Basil.

She forced in a deep breath—held it—then let it out. Wiped the sweat off her face, and slowly laid back down. The pillow felt chilly, and the sheets had twisted around her legs. She frowned, worked them loose, and rested on her back, counting her breaths and making herself focus on the crackle of the low fire in the hearth.

Tap, tap, tap.

She jolted, her heart pounding again—

The door creaked open, and Mrs. Butterfield entered with a pitcher of steaming water.

"Are you awake, Miss?" she smiled at her. "Just bringing the water for your wash."

Nodding, She sat up, pulling the blankets up to cover herself.

"I'll be back in a moment," Mrs. Butterfield said as she poured the water into Her pitcher. "I'll bring you one of Miss Collingwood's travel dresses, and a hat and coat. Mr. Collingwood says he would like to take the noon train to Oxford. The trip will only take *one* hour, can you imagine? It's one of the fastest trains in the country." Mrs. Butterfield turned and smiled at her again. "And I'll make breakfast for you, don't fret. Take your time getting ready for your journey."

Again, She nodded, and tried to smile in return, but failed. Mrs. Butterfield didn't seem to notice, and left the room.

She could not stop shivering, deep in her bones, even though she sat in a snug train compartment upon a padded seat, her legs wrapped in thick skirts *and* a blanket, wearing gloves, a coat, a scarf and hat. She sat with her fingers interlaced and her hands grasped tightly, staring out the window.

Basil sat across from her, wearing all black again, and a traveling top-hat. His blackthorn walking stick rested against his bench. That morning's copy of the *Times* blocked his upper body from her view.

She had hardly been able to swallow anything during breakfast, but Basil had paid no attention to her—he had been busy sifting through the letters that Mr. Cutworth handed him. Letters from yesterday, that he hadn't attended to due to his patients. Jack had come and settled beside Her, and she found that stroking her fingers through the thick hair at his neck kept her stomach from turning over.

After Basil finished his meal, they had arisen, put on their coats, and called a hansom. The frosty air had struck her face as they stepped outside, and it made her clutch the collar of her coat. She squinted against the brightness of the snow as she picked her way down the slick stairs and followed the snow-covered walkway after Basil, who had achieved the hansom much ahead of her. He had even leaped up into it before her, leaving her to struggle inside by herself.

Basil had brought three letters along with him, which he had read during the bouncy hansom ride, and only put them back inside his coat when they arrived and had to dismount.

At the noisy, bustling station, Basil had purchased tickets, as well as that morning's *London Times*, and the two of them waited in silence once more on the platform, until their gleaming train came thundering up, flooding the low space with clouds of steam and heaves of deep, mechanical bellows—like the breath of a dragon.

Now, they sat alone in a first class compartment, and She gazed out across the snow-covered, rolling landscape and grey sky as it flashed by the window.

"You look white as death. Are you ill?"

Her head came around and her fingers clamped.

Basil had bent down the top half of his newspaper and now stared at her over his spectacles, his brow furrowed.

She stiffly shook her head. His eyes narrowed for a moment, then he loudly folded his paper, set it on the bench next to him and crossed his arms. She sat there under his scrutiny for several minutes, refusing to flinch. Finally, he took off his spectacles, carefully folded them and put them in his coat pocket.

"Are you frightened for some reason?" he asked.

She clenched her jaw, and didn't move. Basil raised his eyebrows for an instant, then frowned more deeply.

"All right, interesting," he mused. "Is there...any way you can conceive of a manner of conveying to me what it is you want with my old professor, and why you couldn't simply go to him on your own?"

She bit the inside of her cheek, gazing back into that cold, penetrating gaze...

And shrugged one shoulder.

"Hm," he grunted, then sighed and glanced out the window. "Well, I'm not certain how I'm going to be of much use to you. And I doubt the professor will have any more luck gleaning information from you than I have."

She had no way to respond, so she forcibly turned her attention to the window once more.

Much sooner than she expected, the conductor came trundling down the aisle, shouting out the station stop: Oxford.

A terrible shudder coursed through her. She ground her teeth—and felt Basil watching her.

The whistle shrieked, the train slowed and finally ground to a halt, hissing and spitting like the giant serpent it was. Basil got up and pushed the compartment door open.

85

On shaking legs, She climbed to her feet and followed him, trying to simply keep breathing.

They worked their way out through the train and then out onto the platform, where again the icy wind hit her like a blow. But this time, it smelled frosty, and utterly clear. Incomparable country air. And as her sight filled with the jagged, pale spires of Oxford, draped in dreamy fog, tears stung her eyes.

"We can walk from here," Basil declared over the noise of all the other passengers disembarking around them, as he buttoned his coat up to his throat. "It's about half a mile, but I am cramped from sitting." And he took off down the platform toward the stairs, and She did her best to keep up with him.

As they traipsed down the wide streets, the clouds lowered and it began to snow. Large, thick flakes, like feathers. She held the collar of her coat closed with both hands, and kept near to Basil's left side. He took long, swift strides, his walking stick flicking out in front and back behind him, briskly tapping down through the snow between each stride, as if he wasn't thinking about its motion at all. His other hand he kept tucked deep into his coat's breast pocket. The snow soon blanketed the top of his hat and his shoulders. She was certain she looked the same.

People passed by all around them, emerging from and ducking into the shops on either side. Many of them carried black umbrellas to shield them from the downpour.

As She and Basil walked up the left side of the street, She turned her head to gaze through the glowing shop windows—shops she knew by heart. She knew the names of every single one, and even the names and faces of the people who owned and worked them.

But she couldn't read single sign.

Soon, they turned up a street that She knew with singular intimacy: Broad Street. The houses here had always reminded her of cathedrals, with their gothic decoration, tall windows, and elegant, pointed stonework.

And there, in the center of the row...

Her stomach clenched hard, and her steps hitched. Basil, however, kept walking.

A tall, pale, magnificent, stoic house, with two others pressed against its sides, as if leaning upon it for support. A slender tower marked its foremost corner, and it boasted a mighty chimney. A curl of smoke puffed from that chimney, and She could smell the pleasant, sweet scent of burning peat—so different from the stench of coal.

She could not control her shaking, now.

And, before she realized it, she had stopped walking.

Basil charged on ahead, taking up his stick and trotting up the stairs and into the entry alcove of that house—and disappearing. She remained on the sidewalk, frozen.

A moment later, Basil's footsteps clattered again, and he hopped back out into the snow, frowning at her.

"What *are* you doing?" he demanded. He pointed his stick at the door. "We're here—this is his house."

She squeezed her collar, her feet locked to the snowy pavement. Basil rolled his eyes.

"All right, would you rather go back to the station and take the train back to London?"

Her heart banged, and she shook her head.

"Very well, come on, then," he waved to her impatiently.

She bent her left knee, lifted her foot...

And took a step forward. Then another. Slowly, she worked her way toward him, until at last she stopped in front of him.

He stared at her—through her—that same analytical frown marking his features.

"Now then," he muttered, and strode up the stairs again. This time, she managed to stay beside him. Their footsteps resounded against the stone—She had long ago memorized the tenor of these particular echoes. When they reached the landing, Basil reached up and sharply rapped on the door with the brass lion-faced knocker. A knocker whose nose She had often rubbed with a smile and a wink.

They stood there for a few moments, Basil's jaw

tightening, and waited.

Rustling inside. The loud *clack* of a latch. And then—

The door swung open.

A middle-aged maid with blonde hair and brown eyes stood inside.

And her gaze instantly fixed on Her.

"Good day, Mary," Basil greeted her promptly. "I'm not certain if you remember me, but my name is Basil Collingwood. I was a pupil of Professor Winchester's. Could you tell me if he is at home today?"

But Mary did not look at him. Did not even act as if she had heard him. Her mouth opened—but she said nothing.

Standing on the landing, petrified, She locked gazes with Mary and stopped breathing.

"Mary?" Basil leaned toward the maid, frowning. "Is Winchester at home? I need to speak with him, as a matter of urgency. Could you kindly let us in?"

Mary gasped. It pulled through her whole body like tearing cloth.

"Victoria?" she cried, her hand flying to her throat. "Victoria Thulin?"

Basil's head came around—he stared at Her, his eyes going wide.

Her heart skipped a beat—

And She nodded.

"Good God!" Mary cried, leaping through the door and throwing her arms around Victoria, crushing her to her chest. "You're alive!"

Victoria wrapped her arms around Mary and fought back tears.

Mary withdrew just a bit, and fervently took Victoria's face in her hands, tears of her own running down her cheeks.

"The professor told us you'd been killed in that coach accident!" she wept, trembling. "We were all so horrified and...and shocked—we didn't know what to do, none of us." She shook her head, and let out a broken laugh. "But here you are! What on *earth* happened to you?"

Victoria's lips parted...

But she could only shake her head.

Mary frowned, bewildered, and looked over to Basil—

"Mr. Collingwood!" she yelped, immediately letting go of Victoria and dabbing her eyes with her apron. "Beg your pardon, sir!"

"Nothing to fear, Mary," he said—low and cautious. "But I'm afraid that...*Miss Thulin*...will be unable to answer any of your questions," he glanced pointedly at Victoria, before looking back to Mary. "Unfortunately, she hasn't uttered a word since I met her myself."

"What?" Mary straightened. "Why ever not?"

"If we might come in, I can tell you and the professor as much as I know," Basil replied.

"Yes, yes!" Mary nodded. "Yes, do come inside out of this wretched weather."

In a matter of moments, they had been bustled inside, down a long carpeted hallway, their coats, hats and scarves whisked away, and then they had been ushered into the green parlor. They sat down next to a roaring fire, which blazed beneath the intimidating mounted head of a snarling grizzly bear. Books surrounded them, as did various ivory artifacts and painted portraits of grave old masters. Daylight filtered in through lace curtains over the front window. A tiger skin sprawled across the floor before the hearth.

Basil and Victoria sat down at the tea table as Mary dashed from the parlor and into the corridor. Once again, Basil's penetrating gaze fell upon Victoria—but it carried something keen, and watchful. Her hands shook underneath the table.

The slamming of doors issued from the depths of the house. Muted cries, sharp shouts, and flurried commands darted up and down the corridors.

And soon, the entire staff spilled into the parlor, out of breath and flushed, almost tripping over each other. Esther the cook; Hattie, Tillie and Deborah, the three house maids; Mr. Harrison the butler, and the thin, black-garbed, starched Mrs. Fletcher, the housekeeper.

"Good lord," Mrs. Fletcher gasped, pressing a hand to

her heart. "Miss Thulin. You're not..."

Battling to regulate her breathing, Victoria shook her head.

"Mr. Collingwood," Mrs. Fletcher said, turning to him, her eyebrows coming together in an almost plaintive manner. "Can you...explain all of this to us?"

"I can't," Basil confessed. "She arrived on my doorstep in London a few days ago, unable to say a word, write or read enough to communicate with me. The most she was able to convey was that she wished to see Professor Winchester." Basil got up, and buttoned his jacket. "How do you know her?"

"She...She grew up here!" Mrs. Fletcher gasped, her eyes shining with sudden tears as she turned to Victoria. "Since she was eleven years old! She was such a bright little girl that Professor Winchester would tutor her in all manner of languages, and music, and mathematics. She wrote stories, and painted illustrations to accompany them—she played concerts for us on the piano, she even learned how to cook almost as well as Esther!"

"And I was happy to teach her, I was!" Esther piped up, wiping away her tears and getting flour all over her face.

"Where had she come from?" Basil demanded.

"She had been beaten with in an inch of her life by the headmistress of one of those horrid country schools," Mrs. Fletcher wrung her hands, her voice trembling. "She escaped and ran away across the moor—and Professor Winchester found her beside the road and brought her home."

"She grew up here?" Basil repeated. "I visited this house regularly while I was at school—I never saw her."

"I'm certain you did, sir," Mrs. Fletcher corrected him. "But she was very shy, and you might not have noticed her. You see, it's been only within the last few years that she's turned into...such a beauty!" And with that, Mrs. Fletcher's resolve broke—

And she rushed up to Victoria, took her in her arms, and held her close. Victoria encircled her waist and fought not to break down sobbing. She heard the maids and Cook exclaim, and Mary begin to cry.

Nobody spoke for a long time. Mrs. Fletcher stroked Victoria's hair, and deep quakes ran through Victoria's body—she couldn't make herself calm down.

Finally, she felt Basil step slightly closer, looming over the two of them like a shadow.

"Mrs. Fletcher," he asked—his tone careful and deep. "Why did you believe Miss Thulin was dead?"

"That is what the professor told us," Mrs. Fletcher sniffed, standing back from Victoria and turning to him. She pulled out a handkerchief and patted her eyes underneath her spectacles. "This past August, he was traveling by coach to Cambridge, and he took Victoria with him. It began raining, and a bridge washed out—the horses broke loose, the carriage upturned and fell into the river. The professor was able to escape, but not the driver. Or...Victoria." Mrs. Fletcher rested her hand on Victoria's head. Victoria's face burned. She ground her teeth, and fixed her attention on her skirts.

"Did he not search for her?" Basil wanted to know.

"He did," Mrs. Fletcher nodded. "But it was night time, you see. And the lamps had gone out."

"How did he get home?" Basil wondered.

"He walked along the road until he came to a village, spent the night at the constable's house, and asked one of his former pupils drive him home."

"Who?"

Mrs. Fletcher shook her head.

"I don't know, sir," she confessed. "I can't remember. It was...rather a trying day."

"Hm," Basil mused, clasping his hands behind his back. Then, he straightened up. "Where is the professor now? I'd like to talk to him."

"I'm afraid he's on the continent, sir."

Victoria's head came up.

"The continent?" Basil repeated.

"Yes, sir," Mrs. Fletcher replied. "He is on sabbatical, you see, and he is taking a lecture tour through Germany, Italy and France. He left not a week after the accident. But he plans to be home at Christmastime, for the Hampton Court Christmas Ball."

Chapter Seven

She swept up the walkway to Pendywick Place, her coat billowing out behind her, her fists closed.

They had offered her tea in Oxford, but she had eaten nothing. They had talked about her over her head, but she had not listened. Hadn't heard a word. Just stared at the tiger skin rug on the floor, going cold down to her marrow.

Then, the clock had struck three. And she had gotten up, strode through the crowd of startled staff, and snatched up her coat, hat, scarf and gloves, and swept out the door. She heard Basil say something hurriedly to Mrs. Fletcher, and clamber after her—she was already dressed and onto the street before she heard him charge down the stairs, and shout at her to know where she was going. She had not turned.

He had caught up with her, forcefully demanding answers, but she had ignored him. She followed their old footprints in the snow all the way back to the train station, climbed the steps of the platform, and then stood bullheadedly by the ticket counter, staring at the wall. Basil again stood over her, but she didn't hear what he barked at her. Finally, he heaved a sigh, jerked out his wallet and ordered two tickets back to London.

All the way back to Town, she had stared out the window, her jaw clamped. Basil had never taken his eyes from her, not once, during the entire journey. But she never returned his gaze.

Now, she pulled open the door to Pendywick Place just as Mrs. Butterfield crossed into the parlor. The housekeeper jumped, almost upsetting a tea tray, and gaped at her.

"Miss! What are you doing back so early?"

Victoria didn't look at her. She leaped up the main stairs two at a time, hiking up her skirt as she did. Basil burst through the front door right after her.

"Mr. Collingwood, what is the matter?" Mrs. Butterfield cried. "Is she all right?"

"Her name is Victoria Thulin, Mrs. Butterfield," Basil shot back. "And I haven't the faintest *idea* what is going on."

Victoria paid no attention, achieving the landing and charging up the next set, pushing through the doorway into the family wing, striding down the hall, finding the next staircase and climbing it rapidly, every step screeching. She got to the servants' floor, went to the little library and hauled herself up the spiral staircase, shoved through the door and entered the tower room.

In the same movement, she pulled off the hat and tossed it on the bed, followed quickly by the coat and gloves.

She then bent and opened the trunk, and pulled out the plain, worn dress she had worn when she arrived.

Heavy, clanking footsteps on the spiral case. The door banged against the inside wall.

"What the devil is going on here?" Basil growled, out of breath. "What are you doing?"

She didn't turn around. She just pulled out her precious satchel from underneath the bed. She laid it on the covers, then bent and drew her own battered coat out of the trunk as well, along with her old straw hat.

"Are you...packing?" he pressed. "Where are you going?"

She didn't acknowledge him.

In one swift motion, he swooped toward her, towering over her right side.

"You and I struck a bargain," he snarled over her head. "Do you remember? You can't leave—not until I've studied and diagnosed your defect. Do you recall that particular stipulation? *I* agreed to take you to Oxford and *you* agreed to remain until I was finished."

She did not lift her head. Instead, she pointed sharply back at the door.

"What?" he snapped. She tugged at her collar, then pointed at her old dress, then back at the door.

"No," she felt him shake his head. "No, no, you *lying guttersnipe*, you are breaking your word."

She faced him, raised her chin and glared straight up into his grey eyes and terrible features. His curly hair was

97

mussed from pulling his hat off so quickly, and his collar hung askew from yanking off his coat. And Victoria firmly crossed her arms.

His eyes flashed.

"So, you believe that since Winchester was not at *home*, you're not bound to your promise," he realized.

She raised her eyebrows and gave him a pointed look, then gestured firmly to the door again.

"And what exactly are you planning to do?" he cried incredulously, throwing his hands out. *"Walk* to the continent, is that it? Alone? Because if your plan is to steal a ride on a train or jump aboard a ship, you *will* be caught— most likely you will be *murdered* or jailed before you ever set foot in France. And for what? You have no way of *finding him*. You cannot read, you cannot write, you cannot even *speak*."

Her cheeks on fire, she forcefully turned away from him and began folding her dress into a tight square, ready to simply ram it into her satchel.

"Winchester will be back in London in a *month*," Basil said cuttingly. "Why have you suddenly decided to chase him to the continent? Something else is afoot here— something that the staff at Winchester's house know nothing about, some *reason* you came to me first and not to him, even though you *obviously* knew exactly where his house was. And according to his entire household, you *clearly* knew how to speak and write *before,* so what changed? What happened?"

She didn't look at him.

Basil lashed out and grabbed her right wrist.

She went still.

"What is it, Victoria Thulin?" he hissed, right in her ear. "I must understand. *Make* me understand."

She turned her head, just minutely, and looked up at him.

Blinked.

Because something lurked there behind the cold in his brilliant eyes. Something unreadable.

She jerked loose of him.

He let go.

She threw her dress aside, picked up her satchel and ripped it open, reached down inside...

And pulled out a single sheet of paper. A paper that had clearly been torn from a notebook. She held frankly it up for him to see, biting her lower lip hard.

He instantly focused on it, with the zeal of a blade.

"What is this?" he whispered. His gaze flicked to hers.

She held it an inch closer to him. Carefully, he reached up and took it in both hands. He stepped around her, up to the window, and held the paper to the light, his attention flying across the lines of written text.

"These are exceptions," he muttered, brow furrowing. "Exceptions to the grammar rules of...a language. A language that looks to be a...hybrid of Russian, Romanian...and some sort of old Gaelic?" He peered at it closer, squinting. Victoria stood with her arms wrapped around herself. He looked at her.

"Is this a *new* language?"

She nodded. He returned to it.

"This handwriting matches that of the note you handed me the other day—Winchester's name. Did you write this?"

She nodded again.

"This...is *your* work," he guessed. She nodded.

"What *is* this?" he held up the paper, bewilderment vivid in his expression. "What's so important about *this* piece of paper? There's clearly more—who has the rest of it?"

She held up three fingers.

"Three?" he frowned. She shook her head.

"W?" he said. "Winchester."

She nodded.

"He does?" His eyebrows raised. "He does—he has the rest of the language?"

She lowered her hand.

"And who tore out this piece?" he asked.

Slowly, she pointed to herself.

He studied it further, his forehead stormy...

Until he caught sight of something in the bottom right corner.

His expression cleared. His face lost all color.

"What is this?" he said faintly. "Is this blood?"

She drew a deep, tight breath. He looked at her. Gaze bright as lightning—and open with confusion.

"What happened?" he breathed.

She shivered.

Then, she closed her eyes, a deep pain galling her throat, and braced herself. She lifted her left hand, made a fist—

And made a swift striking motion to the back of her head.

Then, she made a violent flinging gesture, as if throwing someone down a hill.

Basil stared at her.

"What do you mean?" he pressed, his voice low.

She just stood there, arms at her sides, fists clenched. He looked down at the paper—at the blood in the corner. Then back up at her.

Basil stood still for a moment, then backed away from the window.

"Wait...Wait." He held up a hand and squeezed his eyes shut. "You were in a country school till you were eleven, you escaped and Winchester took you home, and tutored you until you were grown, teaching you all kinds of languages and music and maths, during which time you developed this new language all your own, and then out of *nowhere*, on a trip to Cambridge, he attacks you and takes the entire language from you—but only *after* you've torn out the page, since you bled on it..." He opened his eyes and met hers.

She clenched her teeth, breathing tightly, her eyebrows drawing together as she silently prayed...

"Impossible," he finally stated, hushed. "I *know* Harcourt Winchester. He's my mentor, my friend—he isn't capable of doing something like that, not to a lady, not to anyone. And *why* would he? No, there must be some mistake—you must have made a mistake. It was dark, you didn't see your attacker clearly, someone else—"

She lunged forward and grabbed his hand.

He stopped, startled.

She caught up his long fingers, and lifted them toward her face.

He froze—his breathing unsteadied, he blinked rapidly—

Victoria's grip gentled. She opened her mouth, and slowly, carefully, drew his first two fingers in past her lips, her teeth...

Until his fingertips touched the jagged edge of her severed tongue.

Chapter Eight

Basil stopped breathing.

So did she. And she closed her eyes.

Her grasp loosened, until only her fingertips touched Basil's hand...

And she could count the pulse in his wrist.

Gradually, he withdrew his fingers from her mouth, but then reached and cradled her jaw in a gentle touch between both hands.

"Open your mouth," he whispered. Keeping her eyes squeezed shut, Victoria obeyed, forcing her tense jaw to work, to stretch open, to let the light in, to show him...

He tilted her face toward the window.

"Oh, my God," he breathed; a broken prayer that she could feel through his fingers.

Tears slid from her eyes and trailed down her cheeks. They dripped off her chin, onto his hands.

With a light hint, he urged her mouth closed—and for just an instant, his thumbs ghosted across her lips. Then, he released her.

She opened her eyes.

He backed away and turned, and stood for a moment, his head bowed, his hand over his mouth.

Then, without a word, he strode to the door, and left the room.

Victoria sat on the rug by the fireplace, leaning back against the mantel itself, the fire to her left. Her skirts spread out over her legs, as did the red yarn and her mostly-finished scarf. But for several hours, she had not been able to summon the energy to knit. She simply wound the yarn around and around her fingers, loosed it, and did it again.

The door creaked. She looked up.

Jack pushed his way through and pranced in, his tail wagging.

She smiled, more tears threatening—she swiped at her eyes and held her arms out to the golden dog. He came right up and sat beside her, panting happily, and she petted him, leaning her head against his shoulder.

Soft footsteps. Measured and careful.

Basil stepped inside. He had combed his hair, righted his collar, and changed his jacket. He stopped, and stood with his hands in his trousers pockets, looking down on her.

And the icy barrier in his gaze was gone.

His mouth and brow, still stern—but the cold color of his eyes had warmed, just the slightest—and his eyebrows drew together in a subdued, earnest tension. She looked back at him, her arm wrapped around the dog, waiting.

"Any man who takes away another human being's ability to speak is no friend of mine," Basil declared—deep, even and grave. "Forgive my rude presumptions and remarks these past few days. In all my years of study...I have never encountered that kind of savagery. This..." he gestured weakly to her. "...was the last thing on my mind."

She swallowed hard, and nodded, rubbing Jack's chest. Basil ducked his head.

"I also believe I've worked the rest of it out. Somewhat, anyway." He took a step closer. "Do correct me if I'm wrong. But the answer lies in the Exceptions. That torn page you handed me. You cannot have a coherent language without the exceptions—there are so many sentence structures and words that wouldn't make sense, or would change meanings entirely if a person didn't know the exceptions." He looked at her. "You were trying to break the language. Make it so Winchester wouldn't be able to use it. And, evidenced by the fact that he attacked you, took the language, abandoned you, and then returned to tell all his staff a lie that you were dead—and immediately departed again to take a lecture tour on the continent..." Basil's tone grew hard. "He thinks of it as a code. An unbreakable code.

And he is trying to sell it to the highest bidder in Europe."

Victoria stared at him, stunned.

Then, slowly, she climbed to her feet—

And, her heart leaping to the sky—she nodded.

Basil let out a long sigh. Then, he drew himself up.

"Well. By the time we discover Winchester's itinerary on the continent, he will have returned," he stated. "No use chasing him—best to wait. Meantime, we can make plans to attend the Hampton Court Christmas Ball."

Victoria threw him a confused look. He lifted his eyebrows.

"Winchester will attend," he reminded her. "If he hasn't found a bidder for the code yet, he'll undoubtedly still have it on his person. If I were he, I wouldn't leave it at my hotel, unprotected. Best thing to do will be to confront him there, or steal it back by sleight of hand."

Victoria's eyes went wide.

"Don't worry, I'll be accompanying you." He reached inside his coat and pulled out a letter and cast over it. "I believe I'll go talk to Mycroft Holmes down at my club. He's just returned from the continent—he may have heard something." He glanced at her. "I'll have Mrs. Butterfield bring you some supper. You don't look well." He started toward the door, then stopped, put his hand in another pocket and held out a folded paper to her between two fingers.

"This is yours."

She gulped again, stepped up and took it from him.

Her torn page of exceptions.

"I'll be home later this evening," he told her, and trotted down the stairs, Jack following on his heels.

Victoria sat in the window seat in the parlor, her back toward the fireplace, the morning light shining across her green skirt, and the book spread out in her lap. After breakfast, she had discovered a book of botany, filled with colorful illustrations of plants and flowers. And sitting here, studying them in the quiet, with the crackle of the fire in the background...

Almost made her forget.

Swift footsteps down the hall, accompanied by Jack's clattering. Basil emerged.

"Mr. Cutworth, my coat and hat," he shouted. Then, he saw Victoria. "Do you have suitable shoes for walking?"

She frowned, but nodded.

"Good. Come."

She got up, put the book down, and edged over to him.

"Bring Miss Thulin's things, also!" Basil ordered up the hall.

"Yes, sir!" came the frantic echo. In a few moments, Mr. Cutworth, red-faced, bustled in with an armful of effects, which Basil snatched from him.

"You're coming on a walk with me," Basil said—to Victoria. "The sun has finally returned, the fog has left, and it's time for some exercise, come." And he held her coat open for her.

She stared at him, stunned.

Then, hesitating, she stepped forward, turned around and slipped her arms into the sleeves. He quickly tossed it onto her shoulders and let her button it while he put on his own coat.

"If we're to be confronting Professor Winchester in a little more than a month, you can't be limp and helpless—not the way you were last time." He handed her a hat, then wound his scarf around his neck, tucked it into his coat, and then popped his top hat on. "I know that the fashion in London is for a lady to be pale and feeble, but in your case that will prove to be not only foolishness, but perhaps fatal." He gave her a critical frown. "Your corset isn't too tight, is it?"

"Mr. Collingwood!" Mr. Cutworth exclaimed.

"That will be all, Mr. Cutworth," Basil said without looking at him—and the butler scurried away. Victoria blushed, but she managed to shake her head.

"Good." Basil pulled on his gloves, then started to the door. "You will walk with me every morning, at a man's pace, along with Jack. You'll also start carrying this." He snatched up the other blackthorn cane from the umbrella stand and held it out to her. She didn't move.

"Take it. Keep it as your traveling companion, always."

Reluctantly, she reached out and grasped it.

"It's my sister's, so it should be your height," Basil said, taking up his own. "In no time at all, you'll know how to crack skulls and break eardrums with that stick."

Her mouth fell open, but he looked past her and whistled.

Jack came pelting down the main stairs and jetted into the entryway, skidding to a stop next to Basil.

"All right, we're off," Basil declared, and shoved the door open.

The day had warmed, the snow had melted, and the sun shone down upon the wet cobblestones. Victoria had to squint for a few minutes against the bright light as she trotted to keep up with Basil and Jack. A first, as they strode down the walk, she kept close to Basil's left side—

But then he maneuvered around her, and walked on *her* left, nearest the street. Jack trotted next to her right.

"Heaven's sake, *use* the stick, don't just hold it," Basil urged. "Touch the paving as you walk."

Victoria endeavored to do so—she had never used a walking cane before. Soon, though, it swung with relative ease beside her, and she was able to lift her head and look around.

Brompton Road bustled noisily all around them, flooded with carriages, hansoms, horses and men and women. The shops smelled of delicious foods, bells rang, news boys shouted on corners, and street singers belted their trading tunes.

Victoria almost smiled.

They followed Brompton Road northeast until they reached Knightsbridge Road and turned right—though she only knew it was Knightsbridge because Basil told her. Across the street waited the wide, green stretch of Hyde Park, where she could glimpse many people strolling beneath the much warmer sun. At last they achieved what Basil called "Hyde Park Corner," and turned into the park itself. They passed beneath an impressive stone arch peaked with an angel driving a chariot, and followed the path inward, until the noise of the city faded behind them. The air also smelled fresher here, and the shade of the trees softened the edges of the city.

"We can pick up our pace in the park," Basil said. "Less danger of being murdered by a cab." And he lengthened his stride. Victoria gritted her teeth, hoped she wouldn't faint, and kept up. Jack seemed hardly troubled at all, his curved tail bouncing over his back.

"Basil, old man!"

Basil slowed, and turned to the left. Victoria peered around him...

To see Lord Fredrick Brody, dressed in a grey great-coat and top hat, come trotting up to them.

"Good morning, isn't it a fine day?" Fred beamed at them, sticking out his hand for Basil to shake.

"A bit damp," Basil remarked.

"Yes of course, after that dreadful snow," Fred

acknowledged, then turned his friendly gaze to Victoria and took off his hat. "How are you today, Miss?"

She smiled, and dipped her head.

"I'm afraid she won't be much for conversation, not the moment, anyhow," Basil stated. "But we've found out her name is Victoria Thulin, and she's suffering from a unique case of word-blindness, among other things."

"Word blindness?" Fred gave Victoria a curious look.

"Yes—it's when a person *could* read, and then suddenly cannot," Basil informed him. "Usually due to head trauma."

"Goodness," Fred said gravely.

"Yes, it should prove most interesting," Basil said. "I'm going to write a book on her."

Fred's smile returned.

"Well, she'll be a famous lady, then!"

Victoria couldn't help but smile back at him—his features were so warm.

"Of course," Basil said, as if that were a given. "But at the moment, we're off for a brisk stroll round the park."

"I'd love to join you, but I'm afraid I'm late for a meeting with my brother." Fred put his hat back on. "But I would like to call on Miss Thulin tomorrow afternoon!"

"Certainly," Basil replied, and Fred left them. As soon as he was out of sight, Basil scowled. Victoria looked up at him in surprise.

"Grinning fool," he muttered, starting to walk again. "He shan't. Not if *I'm* busy with her."

Jack huffed. Basil arched an eyebrow at the dog.

"Exactly," he said. Victoria still regarded him with a little bewilderment...

But he lifted his head and started to whistle a fishing tune, flicking his cane out in front of him, and she realized she was just holding hers limply—so she tried to remember how to stride evenly with it again, Jack to one side, Basil Collingwood to the other, and the whole city of London stretched out before them.

To be continued in...

The Mute of Pendywick Place
And the Scarlet Gown

Christmas is forbidden at Pendywick Place. A tragic shadow from Basil Collingwood's past looms over the season. Nevertheless, he plans to take Victoria to the Hampton Court Christmas Ball, to confront his former mentor—and her attempted-murderer— Professor Winchester. If they can steal back Victoria's unbreakable code from him, they may save England itself. If they cannot, it will put all of Europe in grave danger...

An excerpt from Chapter One:

Chapter One

No. 26, Pendy Corner

London

December 9th

1881

Victoria opened her eyes. A chill washed over her whole body. She let out a tight breath...

And it clouded in vapor around her head. She shivered.

"God bless you, poor dears...Oh, such fever...I'm so sorry, sweet girls..."

Victoria reached up and pressed her hand to her forehead, the darkness of her tower bedroom swimming with old memories of a narrow, grey, frozen room...fits of weary coughing... Miss McAvoy wandering like a pale ghost between the rows of metal beds, lit only by the flicker of the candle she held in her left hand...

Victoria turned over, trying to brush all of that away like a cobweb clinging to attic stairs...

The fire in her hearth had gone out.

She swallowed. Her mouth had dried. She shivered again.

Stiffly, she sat up, climbed to her feet, and snatched her thick dressing gown from off the chair. Wrapping it tightly around herself and pushing her long black braid back over her shoulder, she felt her way to the door, hoping that the range fire in the kitchen still burned. Perhaps she could sit close enough to it to keep warm until Mrs. Butterfield came down...

She sneaked as quietly as she could down the iron spiral staircase, lighted in the dark servant's floor, and started toward the main staircase. She had no desire to take the servants' stairs—they would be frozen at this time of the morning.

The low-burning lamps on the walls guided her as she crept downward, sliding her hand on the chilly bannister. She clenched her jaw to keep her teeth from chattering.

At last, she found herself on the slightly-warmer family floor, edged into that hallway and began to turn left...

She paused.

Basil Collingwood, owner of the house and her eccentric mentor, kept his bedroom straight across from where she stood. Its cherry-wood door was shut firmly, and no light shone under the crack. But the door to the right of it...

It hung open. Just a little.

Victoria frowned, an odd tremor running through her.

She had lived here at Pendywick Place a month and some days, and she had never seen that door ajar. She had never heard Mrs. Butterfield the housekeeper, Mr. Cutworth the butler, or Basil himself ever say a word about it. At first, she had assumed that it was a bedroom belonging to Basil's traveling parents, or to his sister, who now lived in France with her husband. But not long after Victoria's arrival, Mrs. Butterfield had pointed out those family members' rooms—and *this* was not among them.

She bit her lip, leaning toward the descending staircase...

But stayed.

A grandfather clock in the master bedroom ticked— faraway and hollow.

She stared at the open crack in that door.

Took a step toward it. Another, then another. Her stocking feet brushed silently on the carpet.

She hesitated, cast a furtive glance up and down the corridor—but the lamplights only swayed sleepily. She gritted her teeth, faced the door again, stretched out a hand, and pushed gently on it.

With a soft whisper of a squeak, it eased away from her. The light from outside ventured in, throwing Victoria's shadow down upon the floor. She tipped forward, peering

115

through the gloom...

And let out a low, long breath.

Read "The Mute of Pendywick Place and the Scarlet Gown"
AS IT IS WRITTEN on Patreon!
https://www.patreon.com/AlydiaRackham

Watch for it in paperback on Amazon!

MORE BOOKS BY ALYDIA RACKHAM

The Beowulf Seeker

The Riddle Walker

Linnet and the Prince

The Paradox Initiative

Christmas Parcel: Sequel to Charles Dickens' A Christmas Carol

The Last Constantin

Scales: A Fresh Telling of Beauty and the Beast

Amatus

Bauldr's Tears: A Retelling of Loki's Fate

Find them all here!:
Website:
http://captainrackham.wixsite.com/alydiarackham

Made in the USA
Lexington, KY
11 May 2017